HUNTING THE MAN IN THE MOON

I'm hwyrion, Tomos a Millie

HUNTING THE MAN IN THE MOON

Dafydd Wyn

y Lolfa

To all children who have been bullied

First impression: 2014

Cover illustration: John Lund

ISBN: 978 1 84771 833 4

Published and printed in Wales
on paper from well-maintained forests by
Y Lolfa Cyf., Talybont, Ceredigion SY24 5HE
e-mail ylolfa@ylolfa.com
website www.ylolfa.com
tel 01970 832 304
fax 832 782

Chapter 1

David knew they were out to get him. They never said anything, but the whirring of their bikes as they came up from behind him on his way home from school was a frequent reminder. One of them had ridden up close to the pavement while David was walking along and had laughed when he turned in alarm. When they ganged up in a corner of the school yard and cast glances in his direction, he was in no doubt as to the topic of their conversation. They were related to him like the opposite points on the school compass. There was him on his solitary walks and there was them always grouped together. There was nobody else that mattered for David, though the yard was buzzing with boys playing touch rugby or kicking a ball around. He tried to put them out of his mind, but it was no use. Even in his favourite corner of the school library at lunchtime, he could not immerse himself in a book without looking up uneasily every time the door opened.

It was David's fear of frogs that brought about the first onslaught. Fish he could cope with on his evenings down at the stream. There was 'Jac Barfog' or 'Bearded Jack', as they called the barbel. It hid under a ledge for most of the day, but when it ventured out into the pool at courting time in the evening, it was fair game. Jack would lie in the current, its whiskers quivering, hoping that its gleaming flanks would attract the attention of a female, but it was the boys who came instead with their guileful hands. Then there was the 'Pen a Bola' or 'Head and Belly' fish, which looked like a tiny whale when it surfaced. David could confidently tickle one of these, knowing that it would drift into his hands to be scooped triumphantly into a jam jar. But who could describe his horror when he sometimes found in his cupped hands a shimmer of bubbly slime and a yellow frog kicking around inside it. David could safely ignore the black toad, though it was more sinister in appearance, for it rarely ventured into the river. It hid away in musty corners, laid its eggs in horse droppings and was seldom seen. The yellow frog, however, haunted the pools where it spawned and, unlike the fish which he tickled, it croaked frighteningly in his hands until he managed to throw it away from him.

It was Stan who first noticed his fear of frogs when they had just started in year seven at Croesdy Comprehensive School. They were in their rubber boots, fishing in pools next to each other in the Cae Helyg stream. Stan was stabbing fish with a fork and dropping them into a bowl at an impressive rate. He had offered David a spare fork but he politely refused because he couldn't bear to see the puncture marks on the skin and the tiny globules of blood on the fish that he had caught. David felt sure that a punctured fish couldn't possibly live for long in a jam jar so he kept on with his tickling. Suddenly, as David was groping for his prey under the bank, he found something swishing around in his cupped hands and to his horror, a frog's eye looked coldly at him as he opened them. David called out in terror as he stumbled backwards, splashing his trousers.

"Hold on, I'm coming!" Stan shouted and, quick as a flash, he was with him. No sooner had the frog fallen back into the water and was taking a few frenzied breast-strokes than Stan had scooped it out. He held it up in one hand, pointing it at David at first in fun and then deliberately as he saw the fear on his face. He squeezed it so that it gasped, its mouth opening and closing and its eyes staring.

David moved backwards, slowly at first, blinking nervously but not daring to take his eyes off the bulging head, till he suddenly tripped over a stone behind him and slipped backwards onto the muddy bank. Stan then brought the frog down towards him, forcing its tongue out with the relentless pressure of his tightening fingers. Now it was beginning to vomit – little drops fell like rain on David's convulsed face. Stan squeezed it against David's lips and he knew that it would choke him if he opened his mouth. David gritted his teeth together in terror, then squirmed around and crept away frantically on hands and knees, hearing Stan laugh mockingly as Alex and Aeron joined him and listened eagerly to his story. David jumped to his feet and ran all the way home.

It was after this incident that his frog nightmares began. David had seen pictures of the frog and locust plagues of Egypt in the children's illustrated Bible; now the frogs came home to haunt him. Dozens of green and slimy frogs would hop around him in his sleep, swelling themselves up, panting and blowing. He got up to his feet on the bed but they were still gaping up at him, and he dared not move in case he trod on one of them and it shrieked. David perched on the headboard, clasping his knees with his hands, but they came still closer, and blew on his toes with their gaping mouths. Then a hand picked one up and pointed it at him, bringing it closer and closer with its dilated eyes staring at him, its mouth opening and closing. It was pressing against his lips with its horny nose, forcing his mouth open and trying to squeeze its way in. He tried to spit it out but it was threatening to choke him as it worked its way into his mouth. David had to force himself to crunch his teeth on the frog to save himself from swallowing it, he could feel the small back breaking in his mouth and heard himself screaming as he awoke. He kicked the sheets away frantically, his body soaked in perspiration.

"What's bothering you, David?" his mother cried,

as she hurried into his room. She placed her cool hand on his forehead as he slumped back onto the bed.

"I had a dream, Mam. Frogs were coming after me."

"Frogs are 'Ych a fi'! You must keep away from the river if you're afraid of frogs."

David could not bear going without his evening walk down to the river but he decided to change his style of fishing as some of the other boys were doing, now that they were in secondary school. His father had given up working at the colliery because of his bad chest but he had gone to the expense of buying David a fishing rod for his eleventh birthday. It was a split cane rod, gleaming in its brown varnish, and was so precious to David that he was reluctant to take it down to the stream. Now he had to use it for it would enable him to fish at a safe distance from the frogs.

Alex, who lived opposite, saw him assembling his rod the next evening as he was passing with a jam jar and a fork on his way to an evening's sport down on the river.

"Cor, that's a beauty of a rod. I'll come with you," he volunteered. "I know of a pool over by Cae Hen, the old field, where there's a trout to be caught."

David hesitated, he had suffered more than enough of Alex's taunts at school that day and it would be more relaxing for him to go on his own. But catching a trout with his new rod would be a prize achievement, and might make the other boys look up to him on the school yard.

"Oh, all right then. Have you got some worms?" David asked.

"No, I haven't been able to find any because it's been so dry," Alex replied, "but as I was out hunting for worms by torchlight last night, I found a few small snails on the cabbage leaves and I've got them here in a jar."

"They should do just as well," David said. "I found a book on angling in the school library which said that trout eat more water snails off the bottom than they do worms, because those only get washed off the bank during a flood."

Alex nodded in deference to David's knowledge, though he wasn't keen on this talk about the school library. He preferred to be out on the yard or round behind the bicycle sheds at lunchtime.

The two of them made their way across the sloping fields to the Cae Hen pool.

"I'll put a snail on the hook," Alex volunteered, "and I'll hold the line till you're ready to cast out since you haven't got a spinning reel."

David took up his position on the bank of the pool, his legs astride, and prepared to cast as Alex threaded the snail onto the hook. He then held the line for David to swing it round.

"Ready!" David called as he prepared to cast but

Alex had dropped the line too soon, the sticky snail stuck to his trousers and the swing of David's rod drove the hook into the cloth. Alex shrieked as the barb scratched his skin and, in his fear, he turned and started running home.

"Hang on, I'll get it out!" David shouted but Alex kept on running and David had to run after him, terrified in case the strain broke his rod. He held it up high as he chased after Alex, giving out line as if he were playing a fish.

Alex kept on running with David in pursuit till they reached the door of Alex's house. Hearing his shouts, Alex's mother rushed out and clasped him in her arms as he sobbed out his version of the story. She turned angrily on David.

"How dare you, David Jones, frighten my Alexander by hooking him in his trousers and playing him as if he were a fish? You must have a warped sense of humour to do such a thing."

"It was an accident, Mrs Edwards. I was only chasing him to get the hook out of his trousers."

"Now it's my turn to do the chasing!" she exclaimed, as she caught hold of the line and hauled David towards her till the tip of his rod was within her reach, then she seized and snapped it. He looked at her in stunned disbelief as she took a scissors out of her apron pocket and released Alex by cutting the line before throwing the wrecked rod tip back at David.

Alex now emerged from behind his mother. “You wait, you scum, till we catch you fishing! Stan knows how to scare you!”

David turned away, fighting back the tears, and walked unsteadily homewards. He hid his broken rod under a pile of old sacks in a corner of the shed and tried to compose himself before entering the house.

“Were you pleased with the new rod?” his father asked when he walked in.

“Oh, it’s a beauty of a rod. Thank you, Dad,” David said, forcing himself to smile.

“Did you catch anything, David?” his mother asked.

“I had a big one on, but it got away,” David replied.

“I bet your mates were impressed,” his father said.

“Yes,” David said hesitantly. “Now if you’ll excuse me, I have to go up to my room to do some homework.”

‘What mates have I got?’ he asked himself bitterly as he went upstairs. It was easier for him not to tell his parents the truth. He couldn’t bear having a sermon from his father or seeing the disappointment on his mother’s face on top of what had happened.

CHAPTER 2

Becky looked peevishly at herself in the mirror. A crop of freckles had come out with the late autumn sun and these seemed to clash with her curly yellow hair.

"Drat, what a mess!" Becky exclaimed, "and today of all days."

She was meeting Gwynfor after school that afternoon and she couldn't do much about her freckles before then. Her mother had passed on to her the family secret for getting rid of freckles but the cure only worked if you got up at sunrise and scooped the morning dew off the grass and up onto your face. You then had to rub it into your skin as you chanted the words of a Welsh charm:

> Haul y bore cwyd y brychni
> Oddi ar fy ngwyneb i.
> [Oh morning sun, raise thou the freckles
> from my face.]

The freckles were supposed to fade away afterwards under her fingers or at least they seemed to get fainter as she peered hopefully at herself in the mirror. Now it was too late for the early morning method, Becky thought angrily, as she glared at the sun shining in at her through the window. Her father had gone to his work and she had to fend for herself as usual that morning. It was at times like these that she both missed and resented her mother. Why had she gone off with that man? Why had she left them?

Gwynfor was to be Becky's first boyfriend and she had been treading the pavement in front of his house night after night. She wore a flowery dress which she had bought with her saved up money on her twelfth birthday that September. At last, he had come out to talk with her and had asked her to meet him after school that evening. She knew it was difficult for Gwynfor because he was fifteen and had just started at the technical college. His friends would be sure to call him a cradle-snatcher when they found out that he was seeing a twelve-year-old girl. It was her first date but she knew the procedure from what she had seen of other girls in the village. A girl would walk once round the rugby pitch with her chosen one and then indulge in a lingering kiss behind the changing rooms before going home in time for tea. Becky only hoped that Gwynfor's mind would be fixed on the longed for kiss and he wouldn't pay too much attention to her freckles.

She contorted her face again in the mirror, allowing herself a little cry, watching a few tears streaking her face. If her mother was with her now, she'd be getting on her nerves by constantly warning her about the risks because Gwynfor was three years older than her. Having someone to worry about her would be some kind of support. Her father didn't seem to mind what she did as long as she kept out of trouble and he was free to go down to the pub for his pint at night. She wiped away her tears, straightened her hair, hitched her bag over her shoulder and was off.

Becky and the local Croesdy children had to walk to school because they lived within a mile's radius. Most of her friends travelled in by bus from the surrounding villages and she envied them the daily journey on which they finished off their homework and shared gossip. Becky frowned as she saw David waiting for her down by the corner. She had left it later than usual before setting off that morning, in the hope that he would have gone but she somehow knew instinctively that he would be lagging behind the others.

"It's nice to have company," he said gratefully, as he bumped his school bag against hers.

Becky didn't answer but jerked her satchel up to her shoulder and hurried on. She thought of the older boys who might be put off from joining her because she was in David's company. He was baggage, she thought, as she brushed past some late pupils but David was still at her side, taking her silence to be a kind of consent. Becky slowed down a little as she began to feel sorry for him. She knew that he couldn't cycle to school with the other boys from the village because his parents couldn't afford to buy him a bike. David's father was out of work and his mother didn't earn much money working at the old people's home. Becky sympathised with David, but why couldn't he just tag on to someone else? She felt that he was cramping her style and would gladly have shrugged him off like a dress that had become too small for her.

Becky didn't want him hanging around her, as Gwynfor might think twice about turning up that evening if he saw her with another boy. Nevertheless, she tried to think of something interesting about which they could talk, but she wasn't into fishing and he didn't know much about make-up.

She put on a smile and looked sideways at him as they strode along. "People will start talking about us, David. We're always walking to school together."

David blushed. "It's nice to have someone to talk to," he said.

Becky compared herself with him as they walked along. She was a robust, well-developed girl for her age, while David was almost as tall but much fatter and didn't have any real muscle on him. His strength lay in the blue depths of those eyes blinking nervously behind the glasses clamped tightly to his head. If only she could stay at home to read every night as he did, instead of roaming the streets with the other girls, she might keep up with him at school. It was his reading that gave him an advantage over her in class.

"What shall we talk about?" she asked brightly. "Clothes, fashions, shops?"

"Has your father been out fishing lately?" David asked.

"He went out on Saturday night but came back too late to tell me his usual hard-luck stories," Becky replied. "Perhaps he didn't get further than the pub and just went fishing in his imagination. But at least I didn't have any messy fish to clean on Sunday morning. Hey, why have those blokes got off their bikes?"

David was startled by her words and looked up to see Alex, Stan and Aeron leaning their bikes against the railings and grinning and chuckling as they waited by the hardware store on the square.

"Here come Dai and Becky, the lovebirds! Look, he can't stop blinking at her! She must have shown him something truly amazing!" Alex exclaimed.

"When's the wedding, Dai?" Stan asked. "I'm sure you'll want me to be your best man. I'll bring some frogs so that we can eat their legs at the wedding feast!"

"Don't pay any attention," David whispered, as he brushed past them ahead of Becky, ignoring an attempted trip by Stan.

"Hey, Dai, haven't you heard about Gwynfor, your

deadly rival?" Alex asked. "Some girls prefer an older man."

David tried to hurry on, but Becky stopped in front of Alex.

"What did you say just now?" she asked quietly.

"I was telling David about your new boyfriend," Alex said lamely.

"Look here, mate, you mind your own business, that's what you'd better do, and you can take this for a start!" shouted the enraged Becky.

She swung her bag and caught Alex across the chest. He stumbled backwards, toppling over his bike and crashing to the floor.

"Come on, you squirts, you're welcome to try it on with me!" the flushed Becky assured the other two, but they were already backing hurriedly away.

"That showed them," David said admiringly, as they continued their journey. "Can I walk home with you tonight, Becky?"

"No, I'm meeting someone," she replied.

David heard calls of 'lover boy' as the other boys cycled past on their way home that evening. They wouldn't dare call him names if Becky was with him, he thought bitterly. One day, he'd make them feel sorry. But how, that was the question?

When he got home, he still felt angry and bothered, so he surveyed his array of toy guns, which had been his chosen presents every birthday. The latest and the most lethal in his arsenal was the airgun, bought for David by his parents after he passed his Grade Three piano examination. He found some half-empty matchboxes left around by his father and, after filling one box with all the matches, he had three empty ones to take outside. He checked to see that there was no-one around and then set up the three boxes on the brick wall behind his house before retreating to a range of five yards. He had the satisfaction of shooting jagged holes in each box till he ran out of pellets, after which he returned, feeling slightly guilty, to his room.

Chapter 3

David had to keep away from the Cae Helyg stream now that his fear of frogs was known to the other boys. He felt cooped up in the evenings, being unable to walk down to his favourite pools in search of a new arrival. He missed the fabulous shape of the 'Bearded Jack' quivering in the current and the chubby 'Head and Belly' fish. These were the prized fish which he had often brought home to live with him as his honoured guests for a few days. He kept his latest fish in a jam jar which he proudly displayed on the window sill. In the days following its capture, he cast admiring glances in its direction as it swam round and round the jar on its endless journey until it began to lose balance. It tried quivering its fins to keep on an even keel, but would turn onto its side and then its back and couldn't be revived even when David took it back to the stream. He'd release it among the stones and try to propel it forward with his hands but it inevitably floated, belly upwards, to the surface and became sticky between his fingers.

David couldn't leave it there in case it infected the live fish, which came out of hiding as soon as he retreated under cover of the trees. They'd poke at it inquisitively with their snouts till he went over to fetch it. He'd take the fish home in the empty jar but even the stray cat wouldn't eat it and it seemed wrong to put his fish in the bin. David had to be satisfied with burying the shrinking body, now dry and as stiff as cardboard, in a corner of the flower bed. Eventually, a line of tiny graves surrounded the daffodils in the spring.

David's fear of frogs kept him that Friday evening from venturing along the woodland paths down by the stream, and he had to content himself with taking a walk along the road to Cwmfferws bridge and looking down at the confluence pool where the Cae Helyg stream ran into the Fferws river. There was always a reddish tint in the water and he remembered how their teacher at primary school had told them about the ironworks further up the valley in Roman times. This had given the Fferws river its name, as 'ferrous' in Latin meant iron.

David now focused on the trout swimming in and out among the rusty tins at the bottom of the pool. They were almost impossible to catch because no matter how carefully a boy might lower a baited hook and wait for a tingle on the line, he'd suddenly see the quick flash of a white belly. The hapless angler could sense even before he wound in the line that half the worm would be gone and he'd see bare steel grinning at him. To get closer to these alluring trout, David climbed over the bridge wall and perched on the concealed ledge beneath. Nobody could see him there, he was in a world of his own, hearing people and cars passing on the road above.

As he was cosily curled up on the ledge on that Friday evening, he heard approaching footsteps and then their voices above him as they leant on the wall.

"I've seen him coming down this way more than once, but then he just disappears," Stan said.

"He probably cuts back on the footpath past the Rhos Colliery," Aeron suggested. "I've seen him, once or twice, hanging around with Ray Williams."

"But Ray is much older than him," Stan said. "He's into girls and I've yet to see Dai turning his head to look at a wiggly bottom."

"No, the only girl he talks to is that Becky and she's more like a nanny to him," Alex agreed. "He'd run a mile if a girl showed him her cards. No, I don't think he and Ray have much in common. We've got to find out what's his little game."

"Why can't we just leave him alone and get on with other things," Aeron said. "All our talk seems to come back to him."

"He reckons he's better than us and we can't possibly put up with that," Alex argued. "We've got to cut him down to size."

"Can't we just ignore him?" Aeron suggested.

"That won't work because he doesn't want to be with us in the first place," Alex said. "He'd rather be in the company of Jim Hawkins and John Ridd."

"Who are they?" Stan asked. "I haven't seen them around."

"No you wouldn't, you nutter. They're the heroes in those books he's always reading," Alex explained. "He's in his own little heaven with them and he doesn't want the likes of us butting in."

"I see what you mean," Stan said. "He reckons that we don't come up to their standard."

"Perhaps he's shy," Aeron suggested, "and we're frightening him off. If we let him be for a while he might come round."

"It's not up to him," Alex insisted. "We're the ones calling the shots and there's no peace for him till he realises that."

"That's right," Stan agreed, "he's better than us in class but we're the bosses out here."

"He's not better than us in class," Alex said angrily. "It's just that he reads more books and sucks up to the teachers. That's how he gets attention."

"Yeah, he's a teacher's pet," Aeron agreed, "but he's miles ahead of us in most subjects, you've got to give him that."

"That's nonsense, when we're asked questions in class, I know the answers but he keeps putting his hand up before I have time to think," Alex said sulkily. "We've got as much brains as him but he gets the answers out first."

"He wouldn't be much good in a knockout quiz where his team-mates voted off the weakest at the end of every round," Stan said. "The others would see him as a threat and they'd dump him before the final."

"That's right," Alex agreed. "Knowing the answers isn't any good if you can't get on with people. He thinks he's on another planet, like the man in the moon."

"Yes, do you remember him telling us in class that stupid story about a man going out to collect firewood on a Sunday?" Stan said, "and as a punishment God threw him, the firewood and his dog up onto the moon."

"That was a good story," Aeron enthused, "and on a clear night when there's a full moon you can still see the man, his firewood and..."

"You don't mean to say that you believe that kind of junk," Alex said angrily, "it's just a load of old moonshine."

"He may be living in a fantasy world," Aeron admitted, "but where's the harm in that?"

"Can't you see that's how he tries to escape from us," Alex argued, "but it's 1969 now and we'll hunt down his man in the moon like those three astronauts did last July."

"Yeah, that's right," Stan said, "I'll be Buzz Aldrin,

you'll be Neil Armstrong and Aeron can be Michael Collins, waiting for us in the spaceship."

"You and I, Stan, will walk on the surface of the moon after the Eagle has landed," Alex enthused. "We'll tramp through Dai's Sea of Tranquillity, we'll take giant steps for mankind and show Dai that we are the bosses!"

"We'd better move on," Aeron said uneasily. "Carrying on and on about him isn't getting us anywhere."

David heard them go and then climbed up from his hiding-place, feeling cold and cramped while anxious thoughts buzzed about in his head. Fortunately, he had the weekend ahead of him to calm his fears, but it could only be a brief respite.

*

It was unusually sunny on that Saturday morning as David sat in his room. He lowered the volume of the radio as he heard the drone of voices from the kitchen below. David knew that his parents were talking about their pet subject and, as he tiptoed to the landing, he heard his father's resentful voice.

"He's always up there reading and he isn't at all interested in coming out to help me with jobs. It's not natural for a boy of his age to be cooped up in his room on such a fine day."

"David told me that he had to stay in to listen to a radio play for his homework," his mother said defensively.

"He's always got some excuse for staying in," his father said. "A boy of his age should be going out with his mates on a Saturday."

"Isn't it safer for him to be at home with us than to be hanging out at street corners with the other boys or smoking up in the park?" his mother argued. "Just look at what fags and the colliery have done to your lungs, Isaac."

"We all used to smoke when we were his age," his father said complacently, "it was part of becoming a man. We'd watch those cowboys smoking on the films and then we'd buy a couple of fags each in the arcade. Sam Loshin would open a large packet of Woodbines and sell them to us for tuppence each."

Cancer nails were not for him, David thought, as he returned to his room and closed the door firmly behind him. Now was the time for him to plunge into his story on *The Crossing of Swords*, the title set for homework. He thought of Gary, the brave and daring detective, battling it out with malicious Paulson in *Galw Gari Tryfan* [Calling Gary Tryfan], the Welsh radio serial. Gary's car was running out of control above the precipice and he and Alec were about to plunge over the edge. He hummed the chilling theme music from Tchaikovsky's symphony that would provide the perfect ending to his story. Then he remembered to his disappointment that the homework wasn't supposed to be handed in for another week.

David frowned as he heard his mother coming up the stairs and braced himself for her entry.

"Is there anything wrong, David, that you're still sitting in here instead of going out to get some fresh air on such a fine Saturday?"

"I've got nobody to go out with, Mam," David replied dejectedly.

"There are some friendly boys around, you know," his mother argued. "I was talking to Mrs Williams, Ffos Cottage, this morning in the village shop and she said it was some time now since you last went up to visit Raymond."

"He's three years older than me," David said shyly. "Ray is in form four and has started studying for his O levels."

"Mrs Williams did mention that Ray had promised to show you how to make a whistle out of a hazel twig," his mother continued.

"Oh well," David conceded, "I might as well go and see how he does it."

David closed his books, arranged them in neat piles and was off. He walked up the road flanked by the old houses set out higgledy-piggledy with the new houses filling the gaps in between them. Then he turned down the lane to Ffos Cottage and came upon Ray practising his golf swing in a field next to the old house.

"You're just in time to do some fielding," Ray said, as he teed up another ball.

For the next twenty minutes, David was running up and down, fielding the balls. He was perspiring but thinking it was good fun until Ray shouted in annoyance as he hacked his golfing iron into a submerged stone.

"Oh no, just look at that," he said, as he showed David the jagged edge. "This iron will gash every ball I hit from now on, so we'd better pack it in till I've had time to file it down. Besides, I'd better get back to my science project."

"Have you got time to show me how to make a whistle?" David asked hurriedly.

"Oh, OK then, but we'll have to be quick," Ray replied, glancing at his watch. "Some friends of mine may be coming along later on. You tear out a hazel wand from the hedge while I fetch a sharp knife from the kitchen."

They separated and David was soon struggling with a hazel branch, bending it to and fro till it snapped off.

"Good man," Ray said, as he rejoined him in the field, "we'll get two or three whistles out of that. Now I'll show you how it's done."

David felt at ease as he stood in the shadow of Ray's tall, manly frame as he cut out a smooth six-inch piece of wood and carved a notch two inches up. He then grooved the bark right round two inches further on and kept twisting till a circular piece worked loose and slid off between his fingers. David looked admiringly at the shiny whiteness beneath.

"Right, we're ready now for stage two," Ray declared, as he cut a mouthpiece at the bottom end, then started grooving the wood up to the notch.

"What are you doing, little boys?" asked a superior female voice.

David almost jumped in shock, so wrapped up was he in watching Ray at work. He turned to see Mandy, with her friends Anna and Sid Jenkins, looking at them mockingly.

"I'm showing David here how to make a whistle," Ray said defensively.

"Can you show me how to blow one?" Mandy asked tantalisingly.

"Yes, by all means, if you let me finish it," Ray replied impatiently, as he continued whittling the top side.

"What are you doing now, big boy?" Anna asked.

"I'm grooving a channel for the airway," Ray replied.

"Oh, that sounds groovy," Anna said, "but some of us are blessed with ready made airways!"

David blushed as they burst out laughing and he

wished they'd go away. He knew that Ray wanted to be left in peace with him so that he could finish the whistle.

"We're not hanging around here all day watching kid stuff," Mandy said impatiently.

"We're off up the tip," Sid said, "we've got a new hide-out up there. Do you fancy coming for a walk, Ray?"

"I've got to get down to my project," Ray said uncertainly, "but I suppose I could come for a short while. I'm nearly done with this whistle."

"You needn't bother to finish it on my account," David said apologetically.

"It's no bother at all," Ray assured him as he slid the tubular bark back on. "Here you are, Dave, you can try it out now," he said, handing him the whistle.

"You can blow it whenever you're in danger, Dai," Mandy said.

"And Tarzan Ray will come running," Anna added.

David didn't really want to blow it in front of them but as Ray looked at him expectantly, he took a deep breath, closed his eyes and blew. A high pitched squeak broke the silence.

"That's not the way to do it!" Mandy shrieked. "Let me have a go."

David flinched as she snatched the whistle from him and watched, slightly sickened, as the girls and then Sid made funny faces as they all blew his whistle in turn.

"Give it back to him and let's go," Ray said curtly as he saw that David felt embarrassed. "See you again, Dave."

Not for a long time, David thought disconsolately, as they linked arms and paired off, leaving him on his own as they made their way up to the tip.

CHAPTER 4

"A goose, that's what you want for Christmas," Uncle Myrdd remarked when he called round that Saturday evening. "Get some dark meat and gravy on your plate."

"But it's only the beginning of October, Myrdd," David's father pointed out, as he handed him a cigarette.

"Tut, tut, Isaac, now's the time to get one and fatten it up, it'll take at least two and a half months to get it into prime condition," Uncle replied, as he lit up and inhaled thoughtfully.

"Anyway, I don't know anyone who breeds geese," Isaac said.

"You know Evans of Cae'r Gors, don't you?" Myrdd continued. "He breeds loads of them down by the marsh and says he's got too many goslings this year. I could bring you one tomorrow morning."

"I don't know if I can afford it," David's father said, "now that I'm out of work. And I'll even have to give up smoking before long," he added, as a fit of coughing made him breathless.

"I could get you a gosling from Evans for a couple of quid, and there's an old rain barrel in my shed which you could borrow for a few months. I'm sure David here won't mind having a feathered friend around the place. What do you think, boy?"

"I suppose I could help you to look after it," David said cautiously.

"You'll enjoy taking care of a goose," his uncle assured him, "and fattening your own bird will give you an economical Christmas dinner."

"But what about the killing, feathering and cleaning out of the goose?" David's father objected. "I haven't been brought up on a farm and I don't know how to do those things."

"You leave that to me and my mate," Uncle said, "and if there's a few slices to spare on Christmas day, we'll help you out."

Uncle Myrdd brought the little gosling the next morning as David and his parents were getting ready for chapel. David heard voices outside and through the window he could see something white flapping under his uncle's arm. As he ventured out, he heard the thunderous noise of a barrel being rolled along the tarmac. Uncle Myrdd's friend, a hefty collier called Dewi, was levering the barrel into the shed and then turning it upright.

"It's a little male goose, a gander," Uncle Myrdd said, holding up the gosling as if it were a baby with which he was playing.

Its brown eyes looked at David over his uncle's

shoulder. He followed the eyes as Myrdd took it over to the barrel and bent, lowering it into the dark depths.

David peered over the edge as the gosling started jumping and fluttering its wings, flapping them feebly against the sides of the barrel till it suddenly gave up and sank to the bottom, its head in its feathers. David wanted to comfort it with his hands but he was wearing his Sunday suit and was afraid of dirtying the sleeves on the sides of the barrel.

"Just leave it in there and give it scraps and water twice a day," his uncle advised. "It can't fly out, as yet, but just in case you have a furry visitor from the Cae Helyg woods, here's some netting wire for you to put over the top."

"Once it puts on weight it won't be able to fly much," Dewi assured them. "It's only at the beginning you have to be on your guard and maybe clip its wings."

"What do we do about cleaning out the barrel?" David asked.

"I wouldn't bother much about that if I were you, boy," Uncle said. "I'd just drop in some straw every week – it'll stamp it down – and let the droppings build up cosily beneath him. They'll come in handy for the onions in the spring."

At this point, the gosling started his high-pitched squawking from the depths of the barrel as if in protest against his planned imprisonment.

David felt he had to speak up again on its behalf.

"Shouldn't he have a run as chickens do?" he asked. "It's not fair on him to be cooped up in the barrel and never see sunlight."

Uncle Myrdd looked at him thoughtfully. "Well, I suppose you could let him out into the garden sometimes. He'd eat all the slugs and save you some food that way but someone will have to be with him all the time. He could squeeze his way through a gap in the hedge and the Cae Helyg fox might be hanging about at that very moment, ready to grab him by the neck."

Dad seemed to know what was in David's mind. "Well there we are, it's up to you, boy, but you'll have to be with him all the time, mind, if you let him out. There won't be any going away to hide your head in a book."

"OK then, I'm off," Dewi said. "Give me a call about a week before Christmas, Myrdd, for him to have time to hang; that's what gives flavour to the meat."

"Yes, I'll need your help," Uncle Myrdd agreed. "He'll be pretty strong by then."

"Come on, you two!" David's mother called impatiently, "it's time we set off for chapel."

*

On Monday evening after school, David hurried home, feeling pleased that it was a fine enough afternoon for him to leave the gosling out of the barrel for the first time. He changed quickly from his school clothes and went out to the shed. As he removed the netting wire from the top of the barrel, the gosling got up on tiptoes and flapped its wings as it looked up at him. It reminded David of the picture of a saint turning into an angel; it seemed to fly upwards from a page in the children's Bible. A name clicked into his mind.

"You've come to us before Martinmas, so we'll call you Martin," he said.

David gingerly lowered his hands down into the barrel and felt around for Martin's body. The gosling struck out at him with its beak and wings and he snatched his hands away. David understood the bird's fear and, as he looked long and steadily into Martin's eyes, its flapping slowed till it became a gentle fluttering.

"Quack, quack, quack," it said as it lifted its wings appealingly.

"We can start talking now," David said, "and if you care to join me, I'll show you around my establishment."

David pushed his hands down close to the sides of the barrel and this time, despite a slight agitation of the wings, he managed to close them on the warm body. He lifted Martin up and out of the barrel, then stroked his head to calm him as he had seen his uncle do. Martin settled, wings resting on his arms, as he slowly carried him out and gently set him down on the damp earth of the back garden. Martin stood there quivering his feathers for a moment and then bent forward to touch the earth with his bill, as if he were the Pope alighting from a plane in a foreign country. After that, what a scrabbling there was as he was reunited with his old playmate! He cast dirt all over the place as he dug into the soil and then seized a lobworm's head in his beak, stretching it like a piece of elastic as he hauled it out. He gobbled it up and looked up smugly at David who stared in dismay at the streaks of dirt on his white feathers.

"How are we going to keep you clean, Martin?" David asked.

He mimicked the gosling's reply. "You'll have to find me a pool in which I can bathe, master."

David was jerked out of his play acting by a harsh voice saying, "He's started talking to himself, he's definitely going bonkers."

Looking up, he saw Alex and Stan watching him over the garden hedge.

"You've had a goose to fatten up for Christmas, have you, Dai?" Stan asked.

"That's about it," David replied.

"Please let us know when you're killing it," Alex said. "It'll be something to look forward to just before Christmas."

They laughed mockingly as they rode away on their bikes and David suddenly felt much colder. Alex's words had gone through him like a knife. He caught hold of Martin and, despite his protests, he took him back to the barrel, replacing the wire firmly on top.

"You'll be safer in there," David assured him as he turned away.

*

"You mean to tell me that you now want a bath for it," his father said at the supper table that evening. "That goose is going to cost me a bomb! Myrdd had to pay Evans the farmer a quid more than he expected, then he claimed that he had to buy Dewi a pint for helping him with the barrel."

"Oh, come on, Isaac, an old bath won't cost you all that much, and I'll be having my pay on Friday," David's mother said. "I'm sure I've seen a second-hand bath being advertised in *The Guardian*. I'll take a look now."

"Well, I suppose I might use the bath afterwards for mixing feed for the tomatoes," David's father admitted. "That'll be your job in the spring, David. You'll have to fill the bath with sheep droppings from off the mountain, add water and then stir the mixture with a stick every time you go up the garden."

"Anything you say, Dad," David agreed, pleased

to think that Martin would soon be able to wash himself.

An old bath was bought later that week and David and his father between them managed to position it at the base of an old apple tree where nothing else would grow. David then connected the hosepipe and filled it up.

"Come and see your swimming pool," he told Martin, as he lifted him out of the barrel and set him down at his feet.

"Quack, quack, quack! You're so good to me, master, I'm beginning to enjoy myself here," mimicked David in reply, as Martin trotted beside him up the garden path.

"I don't suppose you'll need arm-bands," David said as they reached the bath and he gently lifted him onto the rim.

"Quack, quack, quack! Can a goose swim?" Martin replied out of the corner of David's mouth as he wobbled slightly on the edge then balanced himself with a fluttering of his wings.

His head moved up and down excitedly as David steadied him above the water and then lowered him in. The coldness made Martin gasp and flap his wings, splashing David in the process. Then he settled down to paddling round and round his metal pool, his yellow beak seeming to smile in the late evening sunshine.

David suddenly became aware of a shadowy figure

by the hedge. It was Aeron, balancing himself on his bicycle with one hand on a post, and trying to sound helpful.

"I tell you what, Dave, if your goose feels a bit lonely in that bath, I've got a plastic duck at home."

"No thank you, you needn't bother, he'll be all right," David replied.

"It's no trouble at all, I'll bring it down on my bike for you to see if it's any use," Aeron insisted. "My brothers use it as a decoy to lure the wild ducks to our pond but they won't be doing much shooting in the next month or two."

The following evening, Martin had just finished his tour of the garden in David's company and was surging round his bath when Aeron poked his head over the hedge and held out a plastic duck.

"Here you are, you can just pop it in to keep him company but I'd better be with you, just in case."

Aeron went round and came in through the gate and together they approached the bath. David lowered the duck in by the taps behind Martin's back but when he turned round and saw it, he raised his wings in alarm and clacked loudly. He tried to fly up but Aeron spread his jacket batman-like over the bath and managed to keep him down. Martin dropped back into the water and then tried an all-out attack on the plastic duck, striking it with his beak till it was lurching up and down in the water. Finally, he stopped and seemed to lose interest, just nudging it out of the way when it crossed his path.

"Jawch, what a performance," Aeron said, "it was worth fetching the duck just to see that."

"You can have it back, now," David said.

"No, you hang on to it till Christmas – it'll keep him company – and I'll have it back after…" Aeron said hesitantly and, after an embarrassed pause, he was off on his bike.

After what? David asked himself painfully as he carried Martin back to his barrel in the shed. Christmas had always been a magical time for him, a day when he could open those longed-for presents under the tree. But now the word Christmas frightened him. Having Martin on a plate wasn't his idea of a Christmas present.

CHAPTER 5

Mr Glyn Lewis, who was in his first year of teaching at the school, was David's form tutor and also his English teacher. It was in his lessons that David's trouble with 'coup d'état' first began. Mr Lewis was keenly interested in the south of France and took his holidays there as often as he could. French words came into the English lessons at some point every day in that autumn term, for Mr Lewis was going to Cannes over half-term and wanted to polish up his conversational skills. He had become increasingly tanned during the last month from his frequent visits to the sunbeds at the Croesdy Leisure Centre in the company of the French assistant at the school.

"This morning, pupils, we're going to look at Gallicisms," he announced. "These, as you know, are French expressions borrowed by the English language."

"Please sir."

"Yes, what is it, Alex?"

"My mother says you shouldn't be teaching us all this French because it's not one of the 'Three Rs'. She says you should be concentrating on English; that's what you're supposed to teach us."

"Look here, Edwards, you tell your mother on my behalf that you can't teach a language in a vacuum. Just look at all the words that have been borrowed from Latin and French into Welsh and English. Now I'm being up-to-date and progressive by forging important links with the French department at our school. Right, let's begin by checking on the French expressions we've already gone over."

"Please sir!" It was Aeron who next raised his hand after getting a nod from Alex.

"Yes, what's troubling you, Aeron?"

"My father doesn't like the French, sir, because he's a farmer and hates the way they stopped us exporting Welsh beef when the foot-and-mouth epidemic was on. He also got fed up with them during the lamb war. It was all right for them to flood our markets with cheap fruit and dairy products, but when we tried to export Welsh lamb, they stopped the lorries…"

"Be quiet, boy! Lamb and beef disputes are matters for the European courts, not for my language lesson. Anybody else who interrupts will be kept in lunchtime."

"But sir," Alex said, "if you keep us in you won't be able to go for your session on the sunbed with Mademoiselle Poitier."

There was half-stifled laughter as Mr Lewis went red in the face. So his pupils knew of his fondness for going to the Health Centre with Chantelle at lunchtime.

"You'll report to me, Edwards, at the beginning of the lunch hour instead of running off to be first in the dinner queue, and we'll take it from there. Now then, without more ado, let's start on our revision of French phrases, as used in the English language. What is the phrase meaning 'We've experienced this before'?"

David knew the answer immediately but didn't want to be taunted by comments such as 'it's him as usual' and 'he would say that'. He could see that Becky was fiddling excitedly with her hair, a sure sign that she was working her way to an answer. She was like her father's Labrador, swishing his tail to and fro before charging into the bushes to raise a rabbit.

At last, Becky's hand went up. "Is it 'déjà vu', sir?"

"'Déjà vu' it is. Well done, Rebecca, I like a bright pupil," Mr Lewis said, as he threw her a mint. David envied her the generous applause of her friends as she caught it dexterously.

When the dinner bell rang, they all trooped out apart from Alex, who had to stay behind. David saw Mr Lewis glancing impatiently at his watch as he passed him.

They had hardly lined up for the dinner queue when Alex suddenly joined Stan and Aeron near the front despite the protests of those queuing behind.

"I've had a telling off which lasted three minutes," Alex said smugly. "I could see his mind was on other things. He'll be going under the sun lamp any minute now, him and Mam'selle, turning themselves over and over."

"Like pork sausages under the grill," Aeron quipped.

"He'll be getting hot by now," Alex said, "and saying to Mam'selle, 'Allons a la Jacousie,' and she'll be saying 'Calme-toi, monsieur, calme-toi!'"

Even David chuckled as he stood behind them, impressed for once by Alex's humour, but his merriment was soon stopped.

"Some of you might have backed me up when I reminded him that he shouldn't be teaching us all that French," Alex said, as he turned to look pointedly at David.

*

At Registration time that afternoon, they all clustered around Mr Lewis as they loved the sweet smell of his shower gel on his return from the leisure centre. He had recovered his good humour and opened the French phrase book once again towards the end of his form tutorial in the last lesson.

"There are two more Gallicisms which I'd like to check upon. What phrase means that something has been arranged and there's no point in further discussion?"

David knew the answer but he didn't dare raise his hand because of the inevitable jibes. He gave Becky the pleasure of saying 'fait accompli' and getting the applause.

"Well done, Rebecca," Mr Lewis said, giving David a quizzical look.

Alex poked him in the back. "Someone is showing you up, mate," he hissed.

"Finally, we'll reverse the order and do it from French to English this time," Mr Lewis said, glancing at his watch to remind himself that there were only four more minutes left. "What is the meaning of the phrase 'coup d'état'?"

David again waited, not daring to be the first to put his hand up. He was reminded of a story he'd read about the children of an Indian tribe who never answered a question until they all knew the answer. Now he realised how they felt and he might as well behave like a member of that tribe to keep out of trouble, so he glanced expectantly at Becky.

She was on a roll and flushed with success; she raised her hand. "Does it mean a chicken coop, a place where you keep chickens?" she asked.

"No, it does not, Rebecca. You've done well today but I'm afraid you know more about poultry than you do about this particular expression."

David allowed himself to join briefly in the ill-mannered laughter of the others but soon stopped, feeling ashamed, when the red-faced Becky looked over at him.

"Now then," Mr Lewis said, "it's all right for you lot to laugh but can one of you tell me what 'coup d'état' really means?"

There was a yawning silence in the classroom, the sun shone on the crossbeam and then the teacher's glance drifted over to David.

He raised his hand reluctantly. "Is it a phrase which means the overthrow of a ruling figure or elite?" he asked.

"It is indeed, and that answer deserves an extra strong mint," Mr Lewis said as he lobbed him a sweet.

David crunched the mint, tasting the hardness of success between his teeth but hearing from behind him an ominous murmur of 'coup d'état' as the bell rang for the end of the afternoon session.

As he came out of school a few minutes late after visiting the toilet, Alex and his gang were riding round and round the yard on their bikes. He sensed that they were biding their time as they watched the school buses leave. They lined up on their bikes as he walked out through the school gates. Nervously, he crossed the road and then lengthened his stride more confidently as he walked the quarter mile down the hill to the village square. He felt relief as he turned the corner and was out of sight of the school.

David drifted into a daydream as he strode along,

but was rudely awakened by the noise of bicycles whirring up behind him and a shout of 'coup d'état!' as someone swung out a foot in passing and kicked him in the behind. He waved a fist at them as tears of shame and humiliation came to his eyes.

They rode on, exulting in their performance, which they were to repeat every afternoon in the weeks that followed. They'd take it in turns to shout 'coup d'état!' and kick him in the backside. On some afternoons, he'd be half running on his way home from school in his attempts to escape from them, but they'd overtake him easily and one would deliver the 'coup d'état'. On other occasions, he'd wait in the reading corner till he thought that they had left but they would still be there when he came out. They'd have a slow bicycle race round and round the yard after the buses had gone, waiting for him to make his move. Then when David started walking and looked back, he'd see them lined up three abreast with Alex's hand raised, as he waited for David to turn the corner and be out of sight of the school.

Chapter 6

David's only relief from the torment at school came when he got home at night and shut the gate behind him. Letting Martin out into the garden seemed to take his mind off his troubles but even that soon had its perils. Martin would run across the garden, flapping his wings till he almost took off. By now, he could soar up to the height of the hedge and David lived in fear of him clearing it and flying away to the Cae Helyg woods where a fox might lie in wait for him. His father must have heard his desperate shouts one evening as Martin was trying to fly, for he came out and saw what could happen.

"Don't you worry, son, Myrdd and I will fix it," his father said.

Isaac managed to contact Uncle Myrdd and the following evening the two of them came up the garden path with his uncle carrying a pair of clippers.

"Now you hold him firm, Isaac," Myrdd said, as David's father enticed Martin to him with a handful of sweet corn, then grabbed him with both hands and held on.

Martin cast an agonised look in David's direction but by now the two men were going about their business.

Myrdd fanned out one wing, then David heard the click as the end bone was cut off. This was followed by a frenzied shrieking and the wild frustrated beating of Martin's wings. The two men had a hard job holding him but gradually they got the other wing into position; there was another click, followed by a shrill scream and then Martin was released. Now he tried in real earnest to fly away, running at each hedge in turn with his wings beating furiously but without the extra leverage of his wing tips, he barely rose above the ground.

"That's done the trick," Myrdd said complacently, as he stuffed handfuls of quills into his coat pockets. "He should be safe now till he's on your plate at Christmas and I know of a fellow who'll be glad of these plumes for fly-tying, or for his wife's hat, maybe. Who knows, he may buy me a pint or a packet of fags."

They lit up and walked away, laughing and joking, but David felt like shouting 'sadists!' He tried to coax Martin to come to him, but the goose now kept his distance, looking warily at David as he hurried around the hedges, searching for a gap through which he could make his escape. Finally, he came to a stop by the bath and tapped it with his beak, looking mournfully at David. He walked over to him slowly and lifted him as gently as he could, being careful to avoid touching his wounded wings, and set him down in the water.

Martin thrust his bill right under, and blood oozing from the torn ends of his wings stained the ripples. After a few minutes had passed, David became anxious but Martin suddenly lifted his head and snorted, then started swimming bravely around his metal pool.

"Good boy," David said, "they've hurt you but you're not taking it lying down, are you? You're making the best of things and getting on with your life."

*

In desperation, David decided to confide in Becky about the 'coup d'état' as there was no-one else to whom he could talk. His mother worried too much about him already and his father wouldn't want to be bothered. Becky listened patiently on their way to school as he described to her the bicycle attacks but he could see that she had other things on her mind.

"They wouldn't dare do it if I was walking home with you," Becky said, "but I can't because things are getting serious between me and Gwynfor. The only time I can see him is when he gets off the bus. Dad is now keeping an eye on me after he gets home from work and he keeps asking me where I'm going."

"But I thought your father was very easy-going and would let you go out late in the evening with the other girls," David said.

"That's all in the past, now he's heard about

Gwynfor from Alex's mother. The old cow actually told him that she saw me and Gwynfor snogging behind the rugby club changing rooms, but how could she possibly have been there, I ask you? She's just making use of what Alex has been telling her out of spite, but she's made Dad scared stiff of something happening to me."

"I'm so sorry, Becky," David said, "it's all my fault. They've been making up stories to get you into trouble because you stood up for me."

"Oh well, never mind, my shoulders are broad enough," Becky replied. "But what about you, let's talk about your problem. Why don't you go home by a different route? Try cutting across the fields just before you get to the square then they won't be able to follow you on their bikes."

David did as she advised that afternoon, hoping the farmer wouldn't see him and harass him with his shouts of 'Out of that field!' He was in luck, the fields were deserted and he could sense the frustration of the boys behind him as he strode across the grass, and their angry shouts of 'coup d'état' had a hollow ring to them. But the fields down by the river were muddy after rain and though he tried to dodge the puddles, his shoes were caked with yellowish clay when he got home.

His father was leaning on the back wall and was very annoyed when he saw David's muddy boots. "How do you expect your mother to clean those shoes and get them ready for school tomorrow?" he demanded. "Why don't you walk home along the road with the other boys?"

"They keep picking on me, Dad."

"Nonsense boy, you're too soft, that's your trouble. Your mother has kept you for too long under her wing. You give them a few belts and they won't trouble you again."

"But Dad, they gang up against me and I can't stand up to them on my own. They chase me on their bikes and kick me from behind on my way home from school. I can only avoid them by cutting across the fields."

"It's no good running away, boy. I wasn't much good at running when I was at school, so I had to stand and fight."

"But there's three of them and only one of me."

"Pick on the biggest and go for him, try to hit him on the nose, that's how you deal with a bully. You must learn to stand up for yourself. Give them a good taste of their own medicine and they won't come back for more."

Right, David thought, as he went out to the shed and thought ahead to the following evening's attack. He pictured the bikes coming up behind him with their wheels whirring, and the phrase 'a sprag in the wheel' came to his mind. David imagined a stick thrust into the spokes bringing the bike to a halt, sending its rider hurtling over the handlebars. He searched for his broken fishing rod which he had hidden in the shed. A four-foot section of that might do the trick.

*

"Why are you taking your fishing rod to school?" his mother asked him the next morning, as he set off earlier than usual and she saw the butt end of the rod sticking out from under his coat.

"It's needed for a nature study project," David said. "We're having a lesson on how to care for snakes in their environment and I don't want to get too close to them."

"No, indeed," his mother said anxiously, "but you'd better take care that a snake doesn't coil itself around that rod and climb right up it."

"Oh, I'll be flicking it off with the tip."

"Who's organising this 'nature study' as you call it?"

"Mr Lewis, our form tutor."

His mother nodded approvingly. "Mr Lewis told me at parents' evening that he was very impressed with you. He also said that you must speak up in class, David. When you know something, son, you must raise your hand. Don't hide your light under a bushel."

David hurried off on his journey to school and

managed to hide a section of his rod in a part of the hedge near where the attacks usually took place, making sure it was out of sight of passers-by, yet easy enough for him to reach.

He bore their taunts patiently that day. Alex became very annoyed when three of his ink pellets were ignored. He leant forward and whispered viciously, "You wait for the 'coup d'état' tonight."

David half turned and smiled. "I'm looking forward to it," he said.

Alex looked mystified. "He's going bonkers," he said quietly to Stan.

David hung about after school till all the buses had gone just to keep his tormentors in suspense. They rode round the yard in gigantic circles, but a light drizzle began to fall and they were getting tired of waiting. It was then that David started on his solitary walk down to the square, knowing that they wouldn't dare attack him before he was out of sight of the school. He stopped to re-tie his shoelaces and looking back, he saw that they were lining up impatiently on their bicycles. Once round the corner, he hurried to the hedge and retrieved the rod section, then held it close to his body. As he resumed his walk, he heard the whirring of the wheels as they came up behind him.

"It's your turn, Stan!" Alex cried.

Stan lashed out with his foot, shouting, "Coup d'état!"

David turned and jammed his broken rod into the revolving spokes of the wheel, exclaiming, as he did so, "Déjà vu!"

The bike jarred to a halt but Stan carried on over the handlebars, crashing on to the road on his hands and knees and ending up with his head on the pavement. He screamed and then cried and groaned, in too much pain to move.

The other two dismounted and walked back, looking shocked and angry. Alex bent down and whispered something in his ear, then Stan lay absolutely still. Alex laid his hand on Stan's heart for a few seconds, then he turned and shouted at David.

"You've killed him, Dai, you're a murderer! You'll be hanged by the neck till you are dead!"

David dropped his weapon and blundered homewards, hardly knowing where he was going. His father wasn't around when he got home, so he went up to bed and lay there sobbing as he thought of spending the rest of his life in prison. After what seemed like a long time, there was a banging on the front door. He heard raised voices and then his father called him downstairs. David hardly dared go down and when he entered the living room, he expected to see the police ready to arrest him in connection with Stan's murder. A wave of relief swept over him as he saw Stan standing there with his face scratched and bleeding, but still very much alive. He felt like putting his hand on Stan's shoulder, but his feelings of gladness were soon dispelled by Stan's angry father, who was carrying the broken-off section of his fishing rod.

"Just look at what you've done with this weapon to my son!" Stan's father shouted, waving the rod in David's face. "Now I want to see justice done, you must be properly punished for wrecking Stan's bike and almost killing him."

"What have you got to say for yourself, boy?" his father demanded.

"They were shouting abuse and kicking me every night as they cycled past on the way home from school," David said. "I just couldn't put up with any more of it."

"Grow up boy, it was only a harmless little game!" Stan's father exclaimed. "What serious harm could they possibly do you from their bikes? What you did was criminal, and by right I should take you to the police for attempted murder."

"There's no need to call in the police, I'll deal with this," Isaac said hurriedly "I'll show you here and now that no son of mine is allowed to do things like that. And just look at how he's wrecked his fishing rod! My wife and I saved up for months to buy him that rod for his birthday."

"But Dad, it wasn't me that broke the rod in the first place, none of it is my fault, if you only knew…"

"No more of your nonsense, boy, you're always

making excuses for yourself. Not your fault indeed!" His father took off his belt. "Now bend over that table!"

David bent to clutch the far end of the table and quivered as the belt bit six times into his backside. He was so hurt that he just stayed there in a bent position, crying quietly.

"Right, I've seen that justice has been done, so I'll let it go this time," Stan's father said, "but if he touches Stan again, I'll rub your son's face in every cowpat on my farm."

David managed to straighten and turn away from his father. He dragged his feet up to his bedroom, despite the searing pain, and lay there. About an hour later, he heard more shouting, this time between his parents and then the noise of his mother weeping after hearing the story, as she came up the stairs. She entered the room and sat silently at his bedside. At first, he couldn't look at his mother but then he turned to face her on his tear-stained pillow.

"Is there anything you'd like to tell me?" she asked.

"Some boys have been picking on me on my way home from school and I just couldn't take any more. I tried to stand up for myself, as Dad told me. But when their parents complain, he's on their side. I can't win, Mam."

"What is it that makes them pick on you?"

"I don't know. It's something inside me that they

can’t bear. Something which goes back as far as I can remember. I’ve got this feeling that I’m the odd one out and I’m always expecting them to gang up on me. I’m on my own and in suspense, waiting for them to pick on me.”

“Is there anyone in particular who makes trouble for you?”

“Alex is jealous because I’m better than him in class and he keeps stirring up the others against me.”

“His parents are like that. They can’t bear to see you out-shining him at school and they can be cruel,” his mother said. “They lock him up in the ‘cwtsh dan stâr’– the little room under the stairs – when he misbehaves. That probably makes him nastier still and he’s taking out his rage on you.”

“I’m never really on the same wavelength as him and the other boys. I feel as if I’m on my own, on another planet… like the man in the moon.”

“There, there,” his mother said, nursing his head in her hands. “You must try to tell us if there’s something wrong. Your father is sorry now; he was only doing what was expected of him by the neighbours. But I’ve told him what will happen the next time he takes the strap to you when it’s not your fault. I’ll be leaving and taking you with me.”

“Oh Mam, I don’t want to come between you. You can’t possibly leave Dad.”

Chapter 7

David was still taunted by the occasional shout of 'Coup d'état' on the way home from school, but there were no more kicks in his behind. The other boys gave him a wide berth as they cycled past as if he were a wounded dog getting ready to savage their legs. They seemed to concentrate now on giving him a hard time at school.

"David knows about frogs, sir," Alex said, winking at Stan, as they walked over to the school pond for their nature study project. The two of them laughed and slapped each other on the back as they saw the frogs poking their eyes up through the slime like miniature crocodiles.

"You're interested in frogs, are you, David?" Mr Lewis asked. "I expect you keep frogspawn in pots till it turns into tadpoles and then frogs."

"No, I'm not into that kind of thing," David replied.

"He's not into frogs but frogs are into him," Stan sniggered.

"Be quiet, boy!" Mr Lewis snapped, "we're trying to hold a civilised conversation and we don't have time for your incomprehensible remarks. Right, pay attention, all of you! We're studying pond life, so we'll start off with these frogs. They have to leave their ponds at this time of year because the water is getting colder. They'll take any risks to get to suitable places to hibernate and it's not unusual to see hundreds of them flattened by the traffic as they cross roads to get to their winter habitats."

"They should have a lollipop lady to guide them across," Aeron said.

"David could be the lollipop lady," Alex suggested.

"I could more easily imagine you, Alex, with a skirt and dollops of lipstick on," Mr Lewis commented.

"Sexy Alex, ha, ha, ha!" Aeron laughed.

"Look here, boy! We're studying pond life, not infantile behaviour this morning! These frogs produce spawn, enough for dozens of them to develop into tadpoles," Mr Lewis said, as he bent over to peer into the murky water.

"Did you hear that, David?" Alex whispered, caressing his shoulder then trying to slide his hand over his mouth. "Imagine millions of frogs swarming all over you, desperately trying to get in."

David panicked as Alex's finger slid into the corner of his mouth, and he couldn't stop himself from biting it. Alex gasped in pain then wrung his hand in agonised silence. David tried to focus his eyes on Mr Lewis as he turned to face them.

"What we'll do now is examine a sample of pond slime," he said.

The school secretary poked her head around the corner. "You're wanted on the phone, Mr Lewis!" she called.

The teacher stifled a sigh of relief. A nature study project had seemed a good idea at first, a chance to get some fresh air into his lungs but this form one group on a Friday morning was heavy going. A ten-minute break on the phone would be most welcome.

"Right, I'd like you to talk quietly in your groups about what we've been doing, and I'll want reports back as soon as I return."

Mr Lewis hurried away and David found himself trying to tag on to Becky while the boys grouped themselves around Alex on the other side of the pond. Becky's answers to his discussion type questions were rather sketchy and impatient because she wanted to talk to Sandra about a dress that she had fancied in a Swansea shop. Becky was hoping it would impress Gwynfor but she wanted Sandra's opinion. Her father might let her go shopping in the town on Saturday afternoon while he watched the Swans playing at the Vetch field.

Out of the corner of his eye, David nervously saw Alex showing his bitten finger to the others and he could hear them muttering angrily as they cast indignant glances in his direction.

Five uneasy minutes passed and then Alex raised his voice. "I'd like to remind you over there who seem to be talking about other things," he said, casting a stern glance at David, Becky and Sandra, "that we're supposed to be discussing pond life."

"Oh buzz off, you little twerp. We want to talk about real boys, not newts like you, don't we, Becky?" Sandra said dismissively.

"Is David one of your real boys?" Alex asked.

"Ha, ha, ha!" chortled his cronies.

"Now then," Alex continued, smirking, "since Mr Lewis has been longer on the phone than expected, I think it's up to us to take the initiative. We'll examine some frogs while we're waiting so that valuable council money isn't wasted. In the absence of our teacher, we must try to educate ourselves."

"Let's have our girls' talk somewhere else, Becky," Sandra said, giving David a hostile glance. "We can't be having some creep butting in where he's not wanted."

Becky looked apologetically at David and hesitated for a moment. He desperately hoped that she would stay but she reluctantly walked off with Sandra. David looked apprehensively at the pond where Stan had already got hold of a frog. Aeron then managed to trap two in a corner and, as one of them jumped, Alex caught it in his cap. Aeron squeezed the other one down into the mud till it gave in and then held it up, panting and blowing, in his hand. He turned round and looked ashamedly at David, then threw the frog back into the pond.

"Why did you do that, you nutter?" Alex asked sharply but Aeron didn't reply.

"Oh well, we've got enough left for what we have in mind," Stan said.

"Yes, let's take them round there, Stan, where the light is better, for us to examine them properly before we report back," Alex said.

Alex and Stan advanced towards David, pointing their frogs at him. He backed away, staring into their Gorgon eyes, till he bumped into the wall behind him and was trapped in a corner. David clenched and unclenched his fists and looked around desperately for help, but Becky and Sandra had wandered out of sight for their confidential talk.

"It won't hurt you, honest," Stan said, bringing the frog to within a few inches of David's terrified face as the back of his head came up against the wall.

David felt his eyes swelling like those of the frog throbbing in Stan's hand. The frog held by Alex was also closing in upon him. Suddenly, to his intense relief, he heard Aeron shouting, "Sir is coming!"

"Damn," Stan said, as he and Alex threw their frogs back into the pond.

"What's going on here now?" Mr Lewis demanded as he rejoined them.

“We were trying to help David overcome his fear of frogs, sir,” Stan said.

“To be continued,” Alex added, as he wagged his wounded finger at David.

*

David felt that he had to get out of the house that evening to release his pent-up feelings. As he could no longer go down to the stream, he chose instead to take a hand-line with him and walk along the road to the confluence pool at Cwmfferws as it was getting dark. There he descended to the concrete ledge beneath the bridge and was hidden from prying eyes as he watched the shadowy forms of trout swimming in and out among the tin cans lying on the bottom. He threaded a worm onto a hook and dropped it in, becoming excited as he felt little tugs on the line between his fingers. It was as if the trout were talking to him in the tingling of the line and it was almost as good as catching a fish. Eventually, he lost patience and jerked up the line, but there was no response and half the worm was gone.

Nobody could catch those trout and the local boys had almost given up trying which made it more of a challenge for him as he sat there late in the evening, dangling his hand-line above the darkening water. David felt safe on the ledge as he was hidden from view and he could watch those alluring shapes swimming round and round beneath his feet. Yet his mind returned to his torment by the school pond that morning and Alex's bitten finger. There was no hope of Alex forgetting his injury and David knew that he was biding his time, waiting for a chance to get his revenge.

CHAPTER 8

It was almost half-term and David could hardly wait to escape from the hostility at school to his longed-for holiday at Pantglas. He ticked off the days on the calendar till it was time for him to go to his aunt's house out on the common. His Aunt June was his mother's favourite sister and she always gave him a wonderful welcome when he arrived. A short, plump figure of a woman, she would envelope him in her chubby arms as soon as he entered the whitewashed house. He could feel free and safe for that half-term week at his aunt's house and he could relax in the company of Islwyn, his cousin, and his only true friend. Islwyn was a kindred spirit to whom he could open his heart as they rambled over the common.

After arriving on the bus that Friday evening, David had to spend some time being courteous to his aunt and uncle and passing on messages from home but he could hardly wait to go out with Islwyn, his cousin. At last they were free to walk along their favourite paths and talk incessantly. They visited the tree with its knotted rope swing and peeped into its hollowed out base which they called the 'wolf's lair'. Then they inspected the empty birds' nests in the hedges around the garden and finally there was the long hypnotised gazing down into the well.

"Now it's time for your favourite drink," Islwyn said, as he lowered the bucket into the blackness and brought it up with water slopping over the sides.

"It's heavenly," David said as he tasted the water from a steel cup chained to the well, "it has that unmistakable tang of Pantglas."

But was there a froggy taste to it also? David asked himself as he drank from the cup. He hastily emptied the remaining water back into the well, much to Islwyn's surprise, and they listened to the drops falling like rain into the depths below.

That first evening, there was a lavish supper of home-made bread and cakes, and a tin of salmon, especially opened to celebrate David's arrival. It was even better after dark when he and Islwyn had, supposedly, gone to bed for the night. They held their breaths and listened intently on the landing upstairs till all was quiet, then they slipped downstairs in their pyjamas and hurried out through the back door. They let out Gelert, the dog, and chased him in and out between the gorse bushes in the moonlight.

"OOOOH!" Islwyn wailed as clouds passed over the moon.

*

The next morning, their wanderings inevitably took them down to the river and, though the fishing season had officially finished at the end of September, they took a hook and line with them just in case they saw a fish.

"The 'twps y dail' or the 'foolish ones of the leaves' have come up the river Lliw with the autumn flood," Islwyn said, "and I've seen some lovely fish among them."

These were the sewin or sea trout that came up from the estuary to spawn in the head waters of the Lliw at the end of the fishing season and they were accompanied by the occasional salmon. The mating urge drove them right up into the low clear water where the locals could catch them easily. The boys had to be on their guard while fishing because bailiffs were on the lookout as it was their job to protect the unborn generations carried by the spawning fish.

"There's usually a nice one lying over there beneath the bushes," Islwyn said, as they approached a shady pool.

They took off their shoes and socks and waded painfully over the pebbles till the water was up to the hems of their short trousers. Then they stopped astounded, for there, partly concealed beneath a tree's roots, was the largest fish they had ever seen in the river. It lay motionless, apart from the slight quivering of its fins and a large forked tail which kept it in position. In an awed silence, they retreated to the bank.

"It must be a salmon come up to spawn," Islwyn said. "I've only tasted a fish like that in a tin."

"We'll try for 'John West' with a hook and worm," David decided.

"What about the bailiffs?" Islwyn asked anxiously.

"You stay here as a lookout," David said. "Just give me a signal when there's someone coming and I can easily throw the hook and line into those bushes. Right, let's get some worms."

They turned over a decayed cowpat and managed to grab two worms before they slithered away. David threaded them onto the hook and then held the coiled line in his hand.

"I'll whistle if I see bailiffs coming," Islwyn said, "then you can dump the line and say you were only going in for a paddle."

David waded over the stones till he had positioned himself adjacent to the salmon's lie. He gently threw the baited hook so that it landed a few yards upstream of the salmon and let it drift down, twirling gently in the current, past the fish's nose. David repeated this process at least twenty times but the salmon remained motionless in the stream. It was as if the great fish realised that if it kept its mouth shut it would stay out of trouble.

David retreated gingerly to the bank after his painful

stand on the stones. “It’s so lethargic, so heavy with eggs that it’s not interested in eating anything,” he told Islwyn. “We’ll have to trap it. Have you got something large at home which one of us could hold in front of the fish while the other touches its tail to drive it in?”

“We don’t have anything like that,” Islwyn replied promptly.

“What about that large shopping bag belonging to your mother? We’d only need to borrow it for an hour and she’d be very pleased to have the salmon for supper.”

“But it’ll get wet and soggy,” Islwyn objected.

“We’ll soon dry it out in front of the fire,” David said reassuringly. “If I’m not mistaken, it’s got a string closure which we could pull shut once the fish is in and then it’ll never escape.”

*

Aunt June was cleaning the windows when they returned.

“Can we borrow the shopping bag please, Mam?” Islwyn asked. “We’ve got to collect something and it won’t take long.”

“Make sure you keep it clean,” she said. “I’ll need that bag tomorrow for I’ll be going shopping to Pengelli.”

Back at the pool they set the trap. David lowered the empty bag into position in front of the fish and, at a nod from him, Islwyn touched its tail. The salmon instantly woke from its sleep and surged forward into the bag. David pulled the string tight and clasped the bag to his chest as the salmon thrashed about inside. He staggered backwards over the pebbles and flopped onto the bank.

"Its tail is bursting the seam," Islwyn said anxiously, as the salmon thrashed up and down in the bag. "Let's tip it out, Dave."

David could hardly believe that his cousin was so worried about a shopping bag when they had just caught such a mighty fish but he undid the string top and let it tumble out onto the grass. Its tail caught Islwyn a glancing blow on the side of his face as he tried to protect the bag. The salmon flopped about, getting perilously close to the bank, till David caught hold of a stone in both hands and brought it crashing down on its head. It lay still and at last they could study it properly, touching it wonderingly with their fingers. It had lost the silver shine of the sea and its back was dark in colour after the months spent in the estuary but it was still a salmon, the lord of the stream.

"Hooray!" David shouted triumphantly, as he released his pent-up emotion.

"Hush, there's someone coming," Islwyn warned him.

Looking up, David could see two men rounding

the corner a few hundred yards away and hurrying towards them.

"Quick, it's the bailiffs, let's run!" Islwyn gasped, as he caught hold of the bag. "You'd better leave the salmon here – it's what they're after."

"We're taking 'John West' with us," David said doggedly, as he picked up the prized catch in his arms and started running clumsily after Islwyn. David's lungs heaved for air and his chest was burning after running half the length of the field. He could hear the men closing in on him from behind and Islwyn by now was about twenty yards in front. He turned and looked back desperately at him.

"Throw it into the river, Dave!" Islwyn shouted. "It's our only hope!"

David knew he couldn't get away. He was staggering past a deep pool at the time so he half turned and let go of the salmon. He heard his fish splashing down into the water and stumbled on, half expecting the men to catch hold of him at any moment. David couldn't run much further and turned, panting and blowing, to face his pursuers. To his relief, he saw they were no longer following him for they had slid down the bank and were trying to get hold of the salmon before it got lost in the pool. Too tired to run, he forced himself to walk on as quickly as he could till he caught up with Islwyn.

"They won't bother with us now," Islwyn said, "if

they catch us they'll have to say what they've done with the salmon. They'll be so pleased we've caught such a fine fish for them."

"And we're too young to be prosecuted," David said, starting to feel braver.

"I'm not too sure about that but I'm really worried about the shopping bag," Islwyn said, "it's soggy and the seam has burst open."

"We'll stitch it up easily enough, and if you keep swinging it in the air it'll soon dry out," David assured him. "But I just can't get that salmon out of my mind. It's the biggest fish I've ever caught and I had to throw it away."

They slipped quietly into the house and Islwyn brought a darning needle and brown thread up to the bedroom. David managed to stitch up the burst seam.

"That's fixed. Now it's strong enough to catch another salmon," he said. "We'll have better luck next time."

"The bag is still wet and it's dirty as well," Islwyn pointed out, looking upset.

"Let's put it in the oven," David suggested. "Once it's really dry, we'll be able to rub off the dust."

They sat uneasily on each side of the coal fire, pretending to read the newspapers as Aunt June came in. She sniffed the air, looking rather puzzled.

"What's this smell?" she asked, "I haven't been

cooking today. Is it possible that I've left something in the oven? I'll have a look now."

As she opened the oven, a cloud of smoke billowed out and a smell of burning leather filled the room. She caught hold of the bag then hastily dropped it on the mat in front of the fire.

"My shopping bag! It's ruined, Islwyn, after you promised to take good care of it! I can't say anything to David because he's not my son but you wait till your father comes home and sees this."

The two of them waited in a tense silence for Islwyn's father to return from work. They heard Aunt June telling him the story out in the porch.

"Come with me into the parlour, Islwyn," Uncle John said, after being shown the ruined bag.

David sat there, hearing his uncle's raised voice, followed by Islwyn's muted replies. Islwyn came out with tears in his eyes. He picked up the bag and put it in the bin, then walked out to the garden. David followed and caught up with him by the well.

"I'm sorry about that, it was all my fault," David said. "I only hope I can make it up to you."

"I tried to tell you," Islwyn began but then stopped.

He didn't say anything more as he stared down into the dark water. Then he let the bucket fall with a splash.

Chapter 9

David dreaded going back to school after the half-term holiday. He kept returning in his mind to the week at Pantglas; it had been wonderful being with his cousin despite the unpleasantness caused by the shopping bag. Islwyn had been rather distant after that for a worrying day-and-a-half but they were the best of friends again on the last morning when they woke up. There were the usual expressions of regret on both sides when they parted.

David had felt so relaxed and happy in his cousin's company but on the Monday he would have to face up again to the relentless bullying. His only hope was that Mr Glyn Lewis, his form teacher, would be able to sort them out. Mr Lewis had spent a week in the south of France and might have encountered the kind of criminals which David had seen in *The French Connection*, a recently released film. He imagined Mr Lewis being mugged by two young thieves late at night in a dark alley in Marseilles. One of them had held out a cigarette and asked him for a light, while the other had jumped on him from behind and snatched his wallet. They pushed him to the floor and ran away laughing. That was when David's teacher showed his true mettle as he picked himself up and sprinted after the slinky youth who had taken his wallet. When the going gets tough, the tough get going, David thought approvingly as he imagined his hero in action.

The thief, who looked rather like Alex, ran down an alley with his fair hair streaming out behind him, but Mr Lewis was hot in pursuit and soon catching up with him. The determined teacher made a final sprint and launched himself into a flying tackle which brought the youth crashing down. He lay there shocked and gasping, still hanging on grimly to the wallet. Mr Lewis had to twist the youth's wrist savagely to make him let go of it and the youth screamed as a bone snapped. David's teacher then stuffed the wallet into his pocket and set off in pursuit of the youth's accomplice, who had a good start on him but Mr Lewis wasn't letting the villain get away with his cowardly attack.

The accomplice, who had Stan's thickset build, was already halfway up the stairs of a bridge crossing the railway, with the screams of his friend spurring him on. He had reached the top and was racing over the bridge when Mr Lewis came swinging across on a wire rope left hanging there by the builders. He landed behind the accomplice as he was about to descend the stairs on the other side, and jerked him back by the collar as if he were a runaway horse. Mr Lewis held him up against the metal railings till he started blubbering.

“Please let me go, sir,” he sobbed. “You’ve had your wallet back and you’ve injured my friend.”

“You must be punished for your criminal behaviour,” Mr Lewis insisted, and he hoisted him up till he was leaning back over the side of the bridge and shouting in terror.

“Are you really sorry for what you did?” Mr Lewis continued. “Do you promise never to help someone rob a tourist again?”

“Anything you say, I’m terribly sorry, sir,” the youth moaned, “please let me down.”

“I suppose a murder investigation would keep me too long from my teaching so I’m giving you one more chance, you rat,” Mr Lewis said contemptuously, as he pulled him back and dropped his crumpled frame on the floor. “But bear it in mind when you next think of mugging an innocent pedestrian that it may be me in disguise and the next time I let you go… it will be over the side of the bridge.”

*

After this reassuring vision, David felt confident that Mr Lewis could deal with his tormentors. On the Sunday morning following his return from Pantglas, David attended the chapel communion service in the company of his parents. He wasn’t old enough to take the bread and wine, but he liked to feel part of the Christian community as the adults received their communion. The words of the service stayed in his mind.

"We enter another life when we partake of the body of Christ," the minister said. "He is always with us after that." The minister was there to shake hands with David and his parents as they emerged from the chapel.

"I liked your sermon, especially the part about Jesus always being with us after the communion," David said shyly, and the minister gave him an approving smile.

David changed into his old clothes and hurried out to the shed after returning home from chapel. Martin lifted his wings in greeting as David removed the netting wire covering the barrel. He slid his hands down beneath his snowy whiteness to lift him out and Martin squawked reproachfully because of David's long absence.

"Oh dear, they haven't been looking after you too well, have they," David said as he smelled the mass of droppings at the bottom of the barrel. "Never mind, I'll clean it all out and carry it to the compost heap. It'll be your contribution to the onion bed in the spring."

"Thank you, kind master," David mimicked, as he put Martin down. "I'll have a run round my lovely garden and a bath later."

And run he did, round the hedges, waving his head in the air, his feet barely touching the ground. David was afraid Martin would soar out of the garden at any moment but by now he was too heavy to leave the ground. The goose suddenly seemed to remember that he hadn't tasted a worm for a week, so he settled down to some serious scrabbling in the damp soil. David returned to the shed, tipped the barrel on its side, then set about cleaning it out with the bucket and spade he used for his castle building on the beach. His father saw him at it as he came out.

"You needn't have bothered, son, but there we are, you can add the droppings to the compost heap. We'll spread it out over the garden in the New Year so the frost can get at it."

David had intended to help Martin into the bath after cleaning his barrel but he had managed to jump onto the rim on his own and was balancing there, flapping his wings. Then he hopped in, causing a wave to slop over the sides. The bath by now had become rather small for him and he had to close his wings before he could turn. He swam round and round his narrowing circle as if performing a dance.

David heard voices behind him and turning he saw his father and his Uncle Myrdd walking up the garden path.

"He's in fine form with you, David," Uncle Myrdd said approvingly, as he looked at Martin squeezing his way around the bath.

"He's a bit slow in putting on weight," his father complained.

"Isaac, Isaac, it's quality that counts not quantity," Myrdd said reproachfully. "David is right to exercise him. Good lean meat is what you want, man, not a load of fat swimming around in the roasting tin."

David felt sickened by their talk and went over to the bath. He stroked Martin's back. "Don't you worry," he said comfortingly. "It'll be over very quickly and you won't feel much pain. Then you'll always be with us in spirit after that."

As soon as his uncle and father had gone, he caught hold of Martin and carried him back to his barrel. "You'll be safer in here," he said, as he replaced the wire over the top.

He couldn't settle down to his school work that evening and after tea he went down to Cwmfferws bridge and snuggled into his corner on the hidden ledge. It was already starting to get dark and he could no longer see the magical shapes of trout in the pool beneath, but he could hear the occasional slosh on the surface as one rose from the depths. David felt himself nodding off to sleep and then was jerked awake by the sound of a fish jumping beneath his feet. Just in time, he thought apprehensively, for he was beginning to slide over the edge. He got up stiffly and made his way home. It was still rather early to enter the house so he walked round to the shed in the semi-darkness.

He entered and listened to Martin breathing deeply in his sleep. David touched the side of the barrel and felt comforted.

Chapter 10

David still felt happy that Monday morning after his half-term holiday and he tried to assure himself that Mr Lewis was gaining in experience and was now firmly in control of his class. The pupils and their enthusiastic young teacher had been in good spirits in the tutorial lesson after Registration, and David had noted approvingly the efficient manner in which Mr Lewis had managed to keep them at their work. The mood of the class, however, soon changed after they had been cooped up in school during the rainy lunch hour and the English lesson at the end of that Monday afternoon became increasingly noisy.

Mr Lewis had to raise his voice while revising the use of the semicolon. "It indicates a pause longer than a comma and shorter than a full stop, and is sometimes useful for adding on a piece of information to a sentence," he told them. "Can one of you invent a sentence in which a semicolon is used?"

David remembered what his mother had said about the importance of speaking up in class, so he bravely raised his hand despite the mutterings of 'Trust him'.

"Yes, David," Mr Lewis said encouragingly.

“The teacher dealt firmly with his unruly pupils; he wasn’t going to put up with any nonsense from them,” David said confidently, despite the whispered ‘creep’ from Alex sitting beside Stan in the back row.

“That’s a most appropriate example of a semicolon,” Mr Lewis said. “Now then, Alex, you seemed to be saying something under your breath. Can you please raise your voice and provide us with another example of how to use the semicolon.”

“‘Mary had a little lamb; she ate it with mint sauce,’ is a sentence with a semicolon,” Alex said, “and I think Stan has another one, sir.”

“Yes, what is it, Stan?” Mr Lewis asked. “Speak up, boy!” he commanded as Stan tittered.

“David had a goose that he ate with cranberry sauce; and wherever David went, the goose went too,” Stan said.

“That will do,” the teacher said hurriedly as David turned red with embarrassment and the other boys started laughing. “Now then, I’ve written the beginnings of five sentences on the board under the heading ‘The Use of the Semicolon’ and I want you to complete them in your exercise books and let me know when you’ve finished.”

David tried to look unconcerned but he was trembling with rage as Alex and Stan sneered at him victoriously. No lesson was complete for them if they couldn’t hurt him, he thought bitterly, as he tried to concentrate on demonstrating the use of the semicolon in his sentences.

It was a mild November day but Mr Lewis had made sure the windows and the door were shut. Perhaps he was afraid that the headmaster was prowling around outside. Teachers in neighbouring rooms had complained just before half-term about the noise coming from one of his teaching groups. David had caught a glimpse through a window of the headmaster's bald head earlier on in the lesson but by now he couldn't see outside because the window panes were steamed up with condensation.

"It's getting awfully stuffy in here, sir, and we can't see out," Aeron complained after getting a nod from Alex. "Would you like me to climb up onto the desks to open the windows?"

"No, I wouldn't, Aeron. The last time you did that, I seem to recall you trampling over those girls' books and I had to give them new ones."

"Why don't you ask Becky to stand on her desk to open a window, sir?" Alex asked. "That should give us a good view!"

Becky stood up threateningly. "If you're not going to deal with him, sir, please let me have a go."

"Sit down this instant, girl!" Mr Lewis snapped.

Becky glared murderously at Alex, who hurriedly retreated behind his book, then with a defiant toss of her head, she sat down.

The class finally got on with their writing and David's confidence returned as he completed the exercise and received an approving comment from Mr Lewis as he came round to glance at the work of those who had finished.

"Right, I expect the remainder of you to complete those sentences by next lesson, and pity help anyone who hasn't done them properly," Mr Lewis declared, as he looked pointedly at Alex and Stan. "In addition to which, I want you to note in your homework diaries that by a week today, I'll want you to write a four-hundred-word essay on the subject of 'My Best Friend'."

"I'll write about you, Stan," Alex promised as the bell rang at the end of the afternoon session, "but someone here present is going to find it very difficult to find a friend he can write about," he added, looking meaningfully at David.

David pondered over this remark as he lingered by his desk. His mind usually started racing once a written assignment had been set; he'd be mentally gathering ideas but now there was a yawning gap. Yet he knew that apart from his cousin, he only had one true friend and choosing to write about Martin might show Mr Lewis how much he was in need of companionship. David tried to calm himself after the turbulent lesson by a careful re-arrangement of his books and pencil case before following the others out of the classroom.

As he emerged from the school, he could see Alex, Stan and Aeron grouped around the exit as the teachers' cars pulled out and he expected further taunts concerning his choice of essay. Yet he soon realised from what he overheard that they had another target in mind that afternoon.

"He must be changing his tactics with Mam'selle and taking her to the leisure centre after school instead of in the lunch hour," David heard Alex say to the other boys standing beside him. "Let's give them a good send-off."

You'll do so at your peril, David thought, as his teacher's imagined heroics in Marseilles came to his mind. He watched as Mr Lewis reversed his car from the parking bay with the French assistant simpering and laughing beside him. The boys started cheering as he drove up to the gates.

"Good old sir!" Alex shouted.

"Give her the full throttle!" Stan crowed, as he hid his mouth with his sleeve.

Wait for it, David thought grimly as he stood there, expecting to see the car shuddering to a halt, the door opening and his teacher emerging in a blazing temper. Instead, Mr Lewis pretended not to have heard and drove on with Mam'selle blushing beside him. So much for my hero of Marseilles, David thought bitterly, as he set out on his solitary walk home. I'm not their only victim.

*

David chose not to start his English homework early that evening. After taking Martin for a run around the garden, he felt that he needed a complete change from his school work, so he set off for the Band of Hope, which was the young people's society at the chapel. The others in his year had stopped going when they moved up to secondary school and David realised that being the oldest there might make him appear out of place. Yet he felt safe in the chapel and he could be of assistance to the minister in giving out the hymns or, better still, he might be called upon to help Miss Daniels with her storytelling.

David still enjoyed hearing Miss Daniels telling a story. She had taught him at primary school and had nurtured his love of reading. How he wished that he could return to the security of his early school days when teachers could keep a close watch on what was going on. Bullies like Alex were carefully supervised but at a much larger secondary school, David had to fight his own battles or suffer in silence.

David recalled how he had once been noisy in his sixth year at primary school during the last lesson on a Friday afternoon, and had been punished because of it. It was the lesson in which Miss Daniels always told a story and David had been sent to stand outside the door. She told the story in a low mellow tone and he had pressed himself against the door hoping to hear what she was saying but her voice was indistinct like the murmur of bees in a distant hive. When the others came out, David had asked Aeron to tell him what the story was about, but he had just shrugged his shoulders, saying it was only a story and he hadn't been listening.

David was now back in the safe haven of the Band of Hope and he listened attentively to Miss Daniels as she began telling the story of Gwion Bach, the young herdsman of Ceridwen the witch, who became Taliesin, the great poet. David knew all the turnings of the story but he soon became involved in the plight of the young boy as Miss Daniels cast her familiar spell. He listened entranced as she described how Ceridwen gathered the ingredients for her cauldron and mixed the potion which would make 'Morfran', meaning sea-crow, which was the name of her ugly and backward son, into a handsome and imaginative boy.

"Let's have some action," Miss Daniels said, and to David's delight, she suddenly came over to him, caught hold of his hand and led him out onto the floor. He found himself mimicking the actions of Gwion, the little herdsman, as he stirred the cauldron for his mistress till suddenly the mixture boiled over and three burning drops fell on his fingers. Gwion instinctively thrust his fingers into his mouth and at that moment he knew that he had inherited great gifts. He also realised that he would be in desperate trouble when Ceridwen woke up and saw that her son

Morfran was as ugly and stupid as ever, and that the charms intended for him had been stolen. So David took it upon himself to imitate Gwion and fled for his life, running in circles round the other children as fast as his legs could carry him.

Miss Daniels now became Ceridwen, the witch, as she woke up and strode out angrily between her listeners, weaving her way in and out between them as she tucked up her skirt and set off in pursuit. David ran round and round the vestry seats with the children cheering him on. He knew that Ceridwen's long legs were gaining on him and as Miss Daniels leant forward he could feel her hot breath on the back of his neck. He had to make use of his new-found magic before he was consumed by her and suddenly he was imitating the bounding run of a hare, and tearing away from her. It was then that Miss Daniels changed herself into a greyhound and was rapidly gaining upon him as they reached the shore of a great lake painted on the wall.

David was trapped but he called upon his wizardry and became a fish with his behind wiggling like a tail. He surged through the water but Miss Daniels was now an otter, closing in upon him yet again. As he reached the far bank, Miss Daniels was snapping her teeth at his coat-tail but David began waving his arms and became a lark shooting up into the sky. Not to be outdone, Miss Daniels also began flapping her wings and drawing her red scarf around her neck; she became a kite ready to descend upon his back and tear him apart with her talons. David could see a haystack far below so he plummeted down into it, and turned himself into one of the thousands of seeds lying at its base. Miss Daniels, not to be thwarted, now became a hungry hen gobbling up the seeds till she swallowed the one in which David was hidden and was made pregnant by him.

Miss Daniels demonstrated her stomach growing larger and larger as David squatted in front of her till she opened her legs and suggested with a smooth, fluid movement of her hands that she had given birth to him.

"You're such a pretty boy," she said, touching the curls on his forehead as the children cheered and David modestly adjusted his spectacles. "I can't find it in my heart to take my revenge by killing you," Miss Daniels continued, "but neither can I forgive you for stealing my son's intended gifts. I shall have to content myself with stuffing you into a pig's bladder and throwing you into the river."

Miss Daniels took out a white balloon and blew it up above David's head and then motioned that she was enclosing him in it before heaving the skin bag out into the stream. Then she donned a coronet and the next moment she was a prince on horseback coming to his rescue. The audience applauded as the balloon burst with a bang and she picked up David from the ford and set him on the horse behind her.

David put his arms around her and imitated the motions of being carried on horseback to the court of King Maelgwyn of Gwynedd.

"Recite some poetry," she hissed, and David obliged by reciting his favourite lines from 'The Kingfisher' by W.H. Davies.

And, as thy mother's name was Tears
So runs it in thy blood to choose
For haunts the lonely pools, and keep
In company with trees that weep…

"And so Gwion bach became Taliesin, one of the greatest poets of Wales, and as you've seen, he also had magical powers and could change himself into whichever shape best suited him," Miss Daniels announced, as she and David bowed and the children gave them a generous round of applause.

Never had tea and biscuits tasted better for David as he sat in the company of Miss Daniels and the Minister in the chapel vestry. She had enabled him to escape for a magical hour by becoming Taliesin and being able to change into different characters but, on the morrow, he would again be stuck with being David, the unpopular scholar.

Chapter 11

David looked steadily at Martin as he perched on the edge of the bath before taking his evening dip.

"I have to write an essay for homework about my best friend," he said, "and I'd like to portray you. Have you got any helpful suggestions to make?"

Martin quacked and looked up at the clouds above David's head.

"I suppose I could start by describing you physically from the top of your beak to the tip of your tail in the manner of the medieval writers," David said. "Then I could pick out those characteristics which best sum up your character."

"Have you also got some tips for my homework?" asked a voice from behind him and David turned to see Aeron leaning his bike against a post in the hedge.

"It depends on whom you've chosen to write about," David replied.

"I think it'll have to be Alex or else he'll be offended," Aeron replied. "Why don't you write about him as well, Dave? It'll be a way of getting into his good books."

"What makes you think that I want to be on good terms with Alex?" David asked.

"Better a bad friend than a good enemy," Aeron

quoted. "He's always got his knife in you but he'd soon stop that if you paid him one or two compliments. It's better for you to butter him up than have him picking on you all the time."

"Never, never, never will I sink as low as that," David replied.

"OK, it's your funeral, I was only trying to help," Aeron said, as he pushed himself away from the hedge and started cycling back up the road.

David stood there uncertainly after Aeron's departure, and the Minister's words came back to him: 'Christ tells us that we should try to love our enemies and that is the most positive and challenging advice we can possibly have.'

All right, David thought, I'll try to take up this Christian challenge and he started racking his brain for good things he could write about Alex. He began with, 'He enjoys a joke' but then felt obliged to add 'at someone else's expense'. David continued with, 'He's a sociable boy who likes going out with his friends' but then felt compelled to add, 'He is at his happiest when he and his friends can gang up on someone like me.'

David decided that writing positively about Alex was extremely difficult and he couldn't possibly refer to him as a friend. He looked again at Martin, perched regally on the edge of the bath, and he stroked his beak before lowering him into the water.

“You are my closest friend,” he said, “and it’s about you that I’ll be writing my essay.”

Martin quacked approvingly as he swam round and round his bath.

*

On the following Monday, after a reminder from Mr Lewis that he would be taking in their essays at the end of the lesson, David’s class started reading *Anne Frank’s Diary*.

“Prior to reading the diary, I’d like to relate your historical knowledge to this particular novel,” Mr Lewis said. “Mr Pugh, your History teacher, assures me that he has given you a general outline of the persecution of the Jews by the Nazis in German occupied countries during the Second World War. Can one of you name the country in which Anne Frank lived? Yes, Rebecca.”

“Was it in Holland, sir?” Becky asked.

“It was indeed, and can you also tell me how the Nazis forced Anne and her family to identify themselves as Jews?”

“They had to wear armbands bearing the Star of David, the emblem of the Jewish nation,” Becky said.

“Excellent Becky, I like a bright pupil,” Mr Lewis said, as he tossed her an extra strong mint.

“David’s star has been eclipsed by Becky’s moon,” Alex whispered.

“Quiet, you lot!” Mr Lewis barked as the boys around Alex burst out laughing. “Can one of the more intelligent members of this class please tell me how some Jews in Holland responded to this persecution when they saw their fellow Jews being rounded up and sent to concentration camps?”

“Can I answer, sir?” Stan asked, after being nudged by Alex. “I’ve never tasted one of your mints.”

“All right then, let’s see if your answer is worthy of a reward.”

“Did they eavesdrop on the conversations of people searching for them… like someone I know?” Stan asked, as he glanced at David.

“That may be partly true but I need a fuller answer,” Mr Lewis said.

David had gone crimson in his face but he felt obliged to raise his hand in order to put an end to this embarrassing discussion. “Did they go into hiding with the help of Dutch sympathisers?” he asked.

“Yes indeed, David, that’s where our novel begins and you can start reading the first chapter,” Mr Lewis said.

Even the unruly members of the class were soon involved in the opening of the Anne Frank story as David read it with feeling and expression.

“Well read, David,” Mr Lewis said, as he brought the reading to a close with ten minutes remaining of the lesson. “Now we’ll stop there as I’d like to take in the homework.”

“Can we have one or two essays read out before we hand them in, sir?” Stan asked. “Alex has written a brilliant portrayal of me.”

“I enjoy writing about my friends,” Alex said modestly. “It gives me a chance to be humorous without getting into trouble.”

“Yes, by all means,” Mr Lewis said magnanimously. “I have no objection at all to listening to one or two character portraits before I take them in to mark. We’ll start with yours, Alex, since Stan wants the class to hear it.”

Alex straightened himself in his seat and began reading loudly and slowly. “Stan is a likeable and popular boy who enjoys socialising with his friends. We cycle together on our bikes to and from school and we go out in the evenings in search of adventure. Stan is a keen fisherman who holds the record for the largest number of minnows caught in one evening in the Cae Helyg stream. He stabs them with a fork and then drops them into a jam jar. Stan also enjoys catching frogs, which is more than can be said for one member of this class. Stan has tried to help this person to catch frogs but his efforts haven’t been appreciated.”

David felt increasingly annoyed as he listened to sentences directed at him and he felt compelled to raise his hand.

"Do I have to listen to all this?" he asked.

"You must stop reading, Edwards, if you are becoming too personal," Mr Lewis said.

"If the cap fits, that person must wear it," Alex said sulkily. "Anyway, we now want to hear David's portrayal of his best friend."

"Whom have you chosen to write about, David?" Mr Lewis asked.

"I've written about Martin, my goose," David replied, turning red in the face as the class burst out laughing. He added angrily, "Martin has certainly got more intelligence and a nobler nature than Alex."

Alex raised his hand with a triumphant grin on his face. "Do I have to put up with such abuse?" he asked, pretending to wipe away a tear.

"I refuse to put up with such petty squabbling in my class," Mr Lewis said. "Now then, you two can work together for once and make yourselves useful by collecting in the homework before the bell goes."

David felt his face burning as he collected in the books while Alex smirked as he acknowledged the smiles of his cronies.

CHAPTER 12

A month had passed by since half-term and it seemed to David that Mr Lewis had adopted a more traditional approach to his teaching. David had been reading on his own in the library one lunch hour and had overheard a senior member of staff telling Mr Lewis, "You get them down before they get you down" and Mr Lewis seemed to have taken this advice to heart. He was now keeping his pupils' heads down in class which entailed a relentless round of grammar, comprehension and summary, then preparing an essay for homework, which they could start in class. David realised that with such a difficult group, his teacher's main priority was to keep them busy in order to maintain silence in class.

"Right, I don't want to hear another word!" Mr Lewis barked for the third time in a double lesson at the end of a drizzly November afternoon. "You should all be working hard on your comprehension of the 'Caribou Passage', and it is essential for you to write down the answers in full sentences. Please raise your hands when you've finished all ten of them."

After the teacher's lecture, there was a tense silence for a quarter of an hour, interrupted ominously at times by the exaggerated squeaking of a pen or a prolonged fit of coughing. Mr Lewis didn't seem much interested in David's contributions that afternoon but he had promised his mother that he would do his best in class.

David raised his hand reluctantly. "I've finished, sir," he announced.

"Right, I want you to draw a half-page picture of a caribou in your book while the others are completing the exercise and then you can read out your answers," Mr Lewis said, as he afforded himself the luxury of glancing again at his watch.

"Can we do Gallicisms when we've finished, sir?" Stan asked innocently.

"Yes please, Mr Lewis," Aeron added in response to a nudge from Alex. "We can't understand why you've stopped teaching us those French phrases."

"We completed that part of the course before half-term," Mr Lewis said hurriedly, hardly able to keep himself from blushing. "Now I'd like you all to finish off your caribou pictures and then have your red biros out ready to mark the comprehension as David reads out his answers."

"Where does the caribou have its hump, sir?" Alex asked. "Stan here has got it under his belly but I've told him that must be his waterworks under a tuft of hair!"

"Ha, ha, ha!" his cronies chortled as Alex looked around for acknowledgement of his cleverness.

"All right, all right!" Mr Lewis shouted, trying to make himself heard as the noise reached a crescendo. The teacher next door might start knocking on the partition at any moment and he wouldn't be surprised to see the headmaster peering in through the window. It was almost a relief for him when Alex and Stan got to their feet and managed to obtain silence by means of waving their arms and shouting a few threatening words.

"Sorry about that, sir, they got a bit carried away by the caribou's hump," Alex said with a smirk. "Now Stan and I would appreciate it if we could have a little talk about French affairs."

"Well yes, all right then," Mr Lewis said, responding eagerly to the unusual quietness. "I don't suppose there's any harm in brushing up on the use of Gallicisms in English for the last twenty minutes of the lesson."

"That's not quite what we had in mind," Stan said. "We would like to know why you're no longer going with the French assistant to the health centre at lunchtime. You used to smell nice and be in a good mood when you came back."

Mr Lewis stood there transfixed, not knowing whether to become angry at this invasion of his privacy or to answer diplomatically in order to keep the noise down.

He laughed nervously. "Dear me, I never expected

my year seven students to take such an interest in my social life."

At this point, there was a knock on the door and the headmaster entered. He looked around, obviously impressed by the deathly quiet which had descended on the room.

"You seem to have a most interesting lesson going on here, Mr Lewis," the headmaster said, as he looked critically around the class.

"We were just talking about the use of French expressions in English," the teacher said hurriedly.

"A topic after my own heart," the headmaster said approvingly. "I don't expect you'll mind me asking them one little question to see how well up they are on these phrases. Can any of you tell me what is meant by the French expression 'Rite de Passage'?"

There was a yawning silence as almost everyone looked baffled, then David felt a poke in his ribs. "You'd better answer, Dave, if you know what's good for you," Aeron whispered.

David raised his hand and the headmaster looked at him expectantly.

"Does 'Rite de Passage' mean a testing experience for a young person, one which prepares him or her for being an adult?"

The headmaster smiled. "Excellent, I couldn't have put it better myself and there's no need for me to detain you any further. I just wanted to remind you,

Mr Lewis, that you'll be needed as a replacement on bus duty at the end of the day." As he strode out, he gave David an approving glance.

"Now you can see, sir," Alex said, "how it pays to be on good terms with us. It might be a good idea for us to have a little break from written work this afternoon."

"Would you like us, sir, to put our books away quietly and then have an alphabet quiz for the last quarter of an hour?" Stan suggested.

"I'll ask the questions out of a dictionary, Stan will choose people to answer and Aeron will keep the score," Alex said persuasively.

"That way, we won't have people talking out of turn and making a lot of unnecessary noise," Aeron agreed.

"Oh, all right then, since this is the last lesson of the afternoon," Mr Lewis conceded, handing Alex a dictionary. "I suppose an alphabet quiz is good for your vocabulary."

He sat in a corner by the window while Alex and Stan took up their positions behind the teacher's table and Aeron, chalk in hand, stood in front of the blackboard.

"Right, what A would you find in Eve's tart?" Alex asked.

"Yes, Mandy," Stan said.

"Apple," Mandy replied proudly.

"Give that girl a mark, Aeron," Alex ordered. "The next letter is a B. What B is illegitimate?"

"It's your turn to answer, Becky," Stan said.

"Do I have to say that word, sir?" Becky asked, blushing as she looked imploringly at Mr Lewis.

"Oh well, just ask someone else the question," the teacher said wearily.

"Do you know the answer, Stan?" Alex asked.

"I do but I'd rather not say that word," Stan said, trying to blush in imitation of Becky as his friends started laughing.

"Sit down, girl!" Mr Lewis exclaimed as Becky stood up aggressively. She hesitated and looked tearfully at David then sat down again.

"The next letter is a C," Alex said, "but I'll ask general knowledge questions from now on. What C was the surname of Old Scarface and what C was ruled by him? Yes, Mandy."

"His surname was Capone and he was the gang leader in Chicago," she replied eagerly.

"I couldn't have answered better myself," Alex said magnanimously. "Give that girl two marks, Aeron."

David retreated into his reveries while Alex's friends showed off their knowledge in the alphabet quiz. Yet as he sat there brooding he felt increasingly self-conscious and knew that he was about to be picked upon.

"Now it's the letter P," Alex was saying. "What P

means to urinate, and it's David's turn to answer this question."

"Pass water," David said promptly, feeling pleased at seeing the disappointed looks on the faces around him.

"That wasn't the answer I had in mind," Alex said. "Can you please answer in plain English for once instead of using those posh-sounding words."

"We'll have no more of that!" Mr Lewis exclaimed, as he stood up.

"Right, since it's time for us to call a halt to proceedings with a few minutes to go, I'd like Aeron, our scorer, to declare the winner," Alex said

Aeron studied the board. "Mandy is the winner with two correct answers!" he exclaimed.

"I'm sure you'll agree, sir, that she fully deserves to be rewarded with an extra strong mint," Alex said.

"Oh all right then," Mr Lewis agreed, as he tossed her a sweet. "Now I want you all to put your books away quietly."

Mr Lewis was off with the bell like an experienced sprinter, closely followed by his pupils while David lagged behind.

"Did you answer many questions in the English lesson today?" his mother asked him as she prepared his food later that evening.

"Mr Lewis didn't seem particularly interested in hearing what I had to say this afternoon," David replied, as he put his books away. “He was fully occupied with some of the others.”

“Well there we are, there are over thirty pupils in your class, and I suppose he has to divide his attention between all of you,” his mother said, as she laid the table.

CHAPTER 13

David gathered from snatches of conversation overheard between lessons that Alex and his friends were going up to the park in the evenings. There they'd hang out with a group of older boys smoking cigarettes and playing cards. David also overheard some mysterious remarks about Anna and Mandy dancing in front of them. Despite his fear, curiosity compelled him to walk through the park on the way to his piano lesson that Thursday evening. He could see them sitting on a bench near the chute; Stan and Aeron were smoking, Alex and Anna were kissing and cuddling but they stopped when they saw him coming. Aeron seemed about to call him over but Alex caught hold of his arm.

David kept on walking, half expecting that one or two insults might be hurled at him as the winding path took him nearer them. It was usually girls who had piano lessons, so he took it for granted that he might be called 'sissy' or 'pansy' among other things. Stan took a last drag at his cigarette, then threw down the stump and suddenly he and Alex, followed reluctantly by Aeron, strode over to stand on the path in front of David. He blinked nervously as they blocked his way.

"We all know you're a great musician and, as your

mother keeps telling mine, you've already passed Grade Three with a merit on the piano," Alex said flatteringly. "So we thought you might like to listen to a little song we've made up in your honour, and give us your frank opinion about its musical virtues."

"Over to you, Mr Conductor," Stan said.

"I've composed the words to the tune of 'Jerusalem' in C minor," Alex announced, as he took up a central position and raised his arms as they gathered in a half circle facing David. "Right, ready boys," Alex said, as he waved a short stick like a baton in his right hand and they started singing:

Last night as I lay sleeping
I dreamt a dream so fair
I slept on Dai Blink's belly
Beside the temple there.

David couldn't stand any more, he pushed Stan aside and blundered along the path, but the song and their laughter rang in his ears all the way to Tommy Piano's house. Never had he been so glad to close the door behind him. Even Tommy's stern face was a relief after the taunts he had endured.

"Have you practised the 'Minuet in G' as I asked you?" Tommy demanded.

"Yes, Mr Owen, I've gone over it… a few times," David replied hesitantly.

"We'll soon find out," Tommy said. "You don't know how lucky you are."

Tommy had lost the tips of three fingers in a colliery accident and he had to improvise with the stumps of his missing fingers when he played the organ at Elim Chapel. He couldn't bear to see lazy pupils not making the most of the perfect hands which God had given them. Tommy kept a wooden ruler at the ready and if a pupil failed to play the notes properly with the tips of his fingers, he would rap him sharply across the knuckles.

David just couldn't concentrate on the 'Minuet in G' after the harassment he had endured on his journey through the park. After only three minutes of playing, Tommy rapped him smartly across the knuckles of his right hand.

"Oh, that hurt, Mr Owen," David protested, wringing his fingers in pain.

"The left hand will be next," Tommy warned him, "and every knuckle will be aching by the time I've finished with you. You carry on with the practising which you should have done at home. I've got a phone call to make."

After five minutes had passed, there was a knock on the door.

"Stop playing, you lazy fellow!" Tommy shouted. "You've wasted enough of my time for tonight."

"It's just that I can't concentrate, Mr Owen," David said.

"Can't concentrate indeed! Go home and tell your parents that and you'll get a real hiding for wasting their money. Off with you and learn to play those pieces properly by next week's lesson or the two of us will be parting company!"

"Have a heart, sir," David begged him. "My parents will be very annoyed if I tell them that I've been sent home early."

"Huh, from what I know of boys, you'll be loafing about up on the rugby pitch till the lesson time is ended. That way, your mam and dad won't find out the truth about what's happened here this evening. Now be gone, and make way for a truly conscientious pupil."

What a shambles. He was going from one disaster to the next, David thought miserably as he fumbled with the door handle to let himself out. Margaret Roberts, one of Tommy's star pupils, brushed past him in the doorway.

"I was so pleased to hear that you could fit me in for an extra lesson, Mr Owen," he heard her say. "It'll be a great help for my Grade Four examination in December."

David couldn't bear the thought of going home early and having a row from his parents. As Tommy had craftily hinted, the easiest way out was for him to hang around somewhere quiet till he could return home at the expected time. He dared not go to the park as the boys would be tormenting him again with their song. David's only safe course of action was to make his way up to the rugby field, but as he rounded the corner into Penygarn Road, Gwynfor almost knocked him over as he came running down the pavement.

No sooner had Gwynfor passed than he skidded to a halt and turned round saying, "Hey you, if anybody asks, you haven't seen me. It'll pay you to remember that I'm Alex's cousin!"

David continued his walk, wondering what Gwynfor was up to. The rugby clubhouse was closed and the field was deserted. He started walking around the touch-line, swinging his arms to release his pent-up energy, but the words of the song with its annoying nickname kept coming back to his mind. It was bad enough being called Dai Blink in the park but he knew from his experience with the 'coup d'état' that from now on the boys would use this nickname to torment him wherever he went.

David recalled that episode in Forrester's novel *The Gun*, in which the French garrison commander realised that his castle was doomed when the cannonball came rolling to his feet. The Dai Blink nickname was to be their cannon, David reflected, their latest weapon in the war against him. He tried to blot out this new threat by making mathematical calculations. He predicted that he would have walked a mile after going round the perimeter of the pitch six times and if he kept up a speed of two miles an hour it would be safe for him to go home after lapping the field twelve times.

"Hey David, come here!"

He looked up to see Becky peeping at him anxiously from behind the rugby club and he walked over.

"Dad's friend called round and they went for a pint, so I slipped out hoping to meet Gwynfor. You haven't seen him by any chance?"

David paused. "There's no sign of him," he said, as he pretended to look round, but his hesitation had made Becky suspicious.

"He's avoiding me, isn't he?" she said bitterly. "He can't have his way so he's dumped me and is having a good time with someone else. Well, he can do what he wants for all I care," she added bravely but then she started crying.

"So you still care for him, Becky," David said protectively, as he put his arm around her shoulders.

"I've got something to tell you but not out here in case someone is snooping around," she said. "We can go into the changing room as the lock is broken and it's where I usually go with Gwynfor."

They made their way in, closing the door behind them.

"Thoughts are buzzing round in my head and I just can't relax," Becky said.

"I'm often like that," David said comfortingly. "You feel as if you're on the defensive all the time."

"Yes, that's it. How can I unwind, Dave?"

"You have to lie on your back on the floor and make your mind go blank," he said. "It's the only way it works."

She looked at the soiled carpet on the floor of the changing room but then she knelt down and turned over on her back.

"Now you can read aloud the words of this poem I've composed to calm myself when I'm feeling agitated," David said, as he handed her a crumpled sheet from his music case.

Becky lay there, her eyes widening as she mouthed the words:

All things unkind
I banish from my mind…

Suddenly the door opened and Aeron stood there, looking curiously at the two of them. Becky scrambled hurriedly to her feet, smoothing down her dress as she did so.

"Sorry to interrupt," Aeron said politely, "I've just come to collect some fags I've hidden here." He went over to the corner, and took out a packet from behind a chair, then he paused and looked sympathetically at them. "Your secret is safe with me, I shan't tell anybody," he said reassuringly, and then he hurried out.

Becky burst into hysterical laughter after his

departure. "As if life isn't complicated enough already, Gwynfor will now start thinking I'm two-timing him."

"Aeron won't tell any one," David assured her. "He doesn't want to make things worse for me. Now that you've calmed down a little, you'll feel better if you tell me what's on your mind."

"Yes, you're the only one I can confide in. Gwynfor wants to become intimate and I'm afraid he'll dump me unless I give in to him."

"You don't want to take any risks," David said uneasily.

"I thought you'd say that and you're absolutely right," Becky said. "Oh well, things may pick up again. Gwynfor has promised to take me to the fair tomorrow night. Are you going?"

"I may pop in," David said. "I love having a wander round but I shan't stay for long."

"Why not, what's bothering you, Dave?"

"I shan't have anyone to hang around with."

"Perhaps you'll make friends with someone at the fair," Becky said brightly. "Gwynfor will be taking me on the Big Dipper, so I'll be looking down on you."

Chapter 14

Loud music was being churned out as David stood on the fringes of the fairground that evening. He could see Alex and Stan mucking about at the coconut stall and Aeron trying his luck at the shooting gallery next door. He heard someone shrieking his name and saw Becky waving at him as she plunged down on the Big Dipper with Gwynfor looking handsome and elated beside her.

"Why if it isn't David Jones," said someone behind him in a friendly voice.

"Robin Williams!" David exclaimed, feeling pleasantly surprised as he recognised a boy whom he hadn't seen for years. Robin had been his desk-mate at primary school but they had lost touch with each other after Robin had gone away to boarding school. David loved reading comics and stories about such schools and would gladly have gone with him but his parents couldn't afford to pay the fees.

"How are things with you?" Robin asked.

"Not too bad," David said, trying to sound cheerful. "And how are you enjoying yourself at Cawdor College?"

"There are plenty of good blokes there and my

rugger is coming along well," Robin replied, "but I miss the village at times."

"Is this your half-term holiday?" David asked.

"Oh no, I've come home for my grandfather's funeral and I thought I'd drop in here for a few minutes when I saw the flashing lights. It's very quiet at my gran's house, now that everyone is in mourning."

"Shall we have a go on the bumpers?" David asked tentatively.

"Yes, why not," Robin said smiling. "They seem quite jolly."

In next to no time, they were buzzing around in their cars, skilfully avoiding each other. Then David caught a glimpse of Alex and Stan racing over.

"Back home for some fun are you Rob?" Stan shouted, as he and Alex jumped the queue for tickets and were soon pursuing them in their cars.

Alex's car passed perilously close to David on the next circuit but he managed to avoid a head-on collision with him. Stan had only one thing in mind and he drove straight into Robin's car with a shuddering bang, causing him to bump his head on the steering wheel. The ride came to an end and David got out and helped Robin to the side as he dabbed at his nose.

"Your friends have a strange sense of humour," Robin said, as he fanned himself with a bloodstained handkerchief. "I'd better be off."

"They're not my friends and I thought that you

might like to join me on the ghost train," David added, as they walked away from the Bumpers. He hoped that his primary school friend would stay with him and Robin seemed impressed when he saw the ghost train hurtling into the tunnel.

"Going through a ghostly tunnel might be quite an adventure," David said encouragingly, "and the train is about to set off."

"Oh well, just one ride then," Robin said, as he heard the screams blending tantalisingly with the music. He looked around warily to make sure that there was no sign of Alex and Stan.

David was pleased to see that the two carriages behind them were empty as they hurriedly got on after paying for their tickets.

"Just made it," Robin said, relaxing a little as they squeezed into their seats.

The train was about to pull away when two boys hurtled into the vacant seats behind them. One of them was clutching a water pistol.

"Ha! Ha! Ha!" Alex and Stan laughed in unison and David caught a glimpse of Robin's shocked white face before the train thundered into the tunnel.

"Help us, David, we're scared," Alex wailed, as he slid his hands over David's shoulders.

"Please protect me, Rob, there's a good chap!" Stan shouted, as he hung on to Robin's collar.

"Can you please tell these imbecile friends of yours

to leave me alone," Robin protested shrilly, trying to free himself from Stan's grip.

"Pack it in, both of you!" David exclaimed but his words were drowned by the screams of the other passengers as an illuminated white ghost reared up above them. Then huge cobwebs and gleaming spiders brushed against them as they wound in and out between the misshapen, laughing faces.

David shrieked in panic as a jet of cold water shot down his back.

"I'm soaked!" Robin gasped, going into convulsions beside him as he suffered a similar soaking.

The ghost train ground to a halt. Alex and Stan were hysterical with laughter as David and Robin clambered out. Robin wanted to hit them but David dragged him away.

"Don't dirty your hands on scum like them, Rob," he advised him. "It's no good bothering with that sort."

"Well I must be off," Robin declared as he straightened his clothes.

"When shall I see you again?" David asked.

"I'll be pretty busy for the next few months but we're sure to bump into each other again when I come back for a few days," Robin said before he hurried away.

David wandered on past the Amusements. In front of him he saw Gwynfor and Becky posing in the hall of mirrors. Gwynfor swept back his sleek black hair and looked weirdly wicked in a long concave mirror but Becky shrieked in alarm as she saw herself in a convex mirror and her distorted shape appeared dwarfish and hugely fat.

David turned to see that Alex and Stan had followed him and were gleefully watching the pair.

"She's going to have a bun in the oven!" Alex chortled.

"She'll drop a pussy under the bridge!" Stan exclaimed.

David looked at Becky who had heard them and was standing there in tears in front of the mirror. Alex gave Gwynfor a knowing smile but he turned away uneasily.

David mustered up his courage and strode forward to take Becky by the arm. "I'll take her home," he told Gwynfor, and then they were followed by catcalls from Alex and Stan as they walked away.

"Thank you for rescuing me, Dave," Becky choked, as she dabbed at her tears. "I'm going through a nightmare and I just have to talk to someone sympathetic."

She snuggled up to him in the doorway of her house and he put his arms around her protectively.

"Gwynfor didn't mean to hurt me," she said, "it's just that I'm not ready for that kind of relationship. It's as much my fault as his."

"And Alex made you feel very embarrassed," David said angrily, as he saw the tears glistening on her face. "He's going to pay for this, I can tell you that now," he added, as he felt the bitterness hardening inside him.

Chapter 15

It was a late November evening, heavy with drizzle and fog. Martin was putting on weight fast. He seemed to fill the barrel and David had to press his wings close to his sides before he could lift him out. His legs were getting well fleshed and three strokes took him from one end of the bath to the other. He gobbled up all the scraps they could give him and seemed to have caught every snail and worm in the garden.

"You're putting on too much weight, it's bad for your heart," David told him anxiously.

"Quack, quack, quack," Martin said, lifting his bill to be stroked.

Apart from tending to Martin that evening, David only had time for a quick walk down to Cwmfferws bridge before it got really dark. He reached his usual place without being seen, then crouched on the ledge, watching the fabulous shapes of trout in the pool beneath. David had taken a little hand line with him just in case the fish were rising and he decided to experiment with a small hook on which he threaded a tiny worm.

"You'll be very clever indeed if you can get away with half of this worm without getting caught," he told the fish now rising to the flies in the pool beneath. David lowered the baited hook but it seemed to go unnoticed as it sank among the rusty cans at the bottom, and jiggling it up and down had no effect.

David tried to vary the size of worm but the fish were just not interested though they were taking the flies that landed on the surface. It was then that a bluebottle fly stuck to the back of his hand, the one holding the line. As it concentrated on extracting a tiny drop of blood, David closed his free hand around its wings. It whirred between his fingers as he pulled up the hook and scuffed off the worm. He then managed to push the hook through the fly and, as it buzzed furiously, he dropped it onto the water beneath. It caused a slight ripple on the surface and then he saw a white shape rising like a torpedo in the semi darkness and taking the buzzing fly so savagely that the line cut into his hand. As the fish turned and dived, he had to let out the line till the last coil was tightening around his wrist. Then the trout jumped repeatedly at the tail of the pool, splashing the darkness into a broken whiteness. David braced himself for that moment when it would drop over the jagged rocks into the pool below, snapping the line. He dreaded feeling at any moment the line going slack in his hand and the disappointment spreading through him.

Suddenly, there was someone wading into the tail of the pool, driving the trout back towards him.

He recognised Aeron's voice as he shouted in the darkness.

"You hang on, Mister, I'll stop it going over!"

Round and round it went in the pool beneath David's feet, diving under the concrete ledges but its surges were becoming fewer and David could take in more and more line as its circling decreased. At last it hung there, turning on its side in the current, twelve feet below him. David crouched there undecided. If he tried pulling it up, the small hook might tear out.

Aeron's voice came to him urgently. "Don't try pulling it up, Mister – it's too heavy – let it come down the current to me. I'll get it by the tail."

As he let it fall back, he heard the voices of Alex and Stan as they joined Aeron. Damn, blast! he thought. Aeron by himself he could cope with, but not that lot with him and he wasn't going to let them have his fish. Suddenly, he was hauling in the trout, pulling it up recklessly, hand over hand till it was only an arm's length away when suddenly the hook tore out of its mouth and it splashed back into the pool.

"Damn, damn, damn!" Aeron shouted. "I've soaked my shoes and trousers and all for nothing. What the heck's wrong with you, mun?"

David turned away and climbed up from the ledge onto the wall and he was about to drop over onto the road and make his escape when a torch was shone full in his face.

"Why, if it isn't our old friend David Jones," he heard Alex say.

There was another bout of swearing from Aeron and a callous laugh from Stan.

"If you knew it was that fat face, you wouldn't have suffered a soaking for him," Stan told Aeron.

"So this is where Dai Blink has been coming for his evening walks," Alex said.

"I told you it was around here he did his disappearing act and all the time he was hiding out on that ledge," Stan said.

"You were listening to everything we had to say about you," Alex told David.

"And you didn't want to have anything to do with your good friends," Stan added sadly.

David scrambled over the wall and hurried away from them, choosing not to hear their mocking laughter but they were coming after him and suddenly they burst into song.

Last night as I lay sleeping
I dreamt a dream so fair
I sat on Dai Blink's belly
Beside the temple there.

David picked up a stone and, turning, he threw it up into the air with all the strength he could muster. He heard it hitting a tree and suddenly went weak at the knees and was relieved that he hadn't thrown it at them. The singing stopped.

"Look out, boys, he's throwing stones at us!" Stan exclaimed.

"Are you all there?" Alex demanded. "If that had hit us they'd have locked you up behind bars and thrown away the key!"

"Where's your sense of humour?" Stan demanded. "What's the harm in a little singing and name-calling?"

"You try putting up with it," David blurted out, as he turned briefly to face them and then he half walked, half ran with their scornful comments fading behind him.

When he got home he had homework to do but wasn't in the mood to get down to it. Bed was his only escape and he lay there dreading the grim morrow in their company.

*

All through the lunch hour on the next day, they were sitting on the wall singing their 'Dai Blink' song over and over again. David tried to keep to the other side of the yard and even went into hiding in the toilets for ten minutes. The moment he came out, he was greeted by a blast of 'Last night as I lay sleeping' and he couldn't shut his ears to it. He tried to persuade himself that the other pupils didn't know what was going on, but soon realised from their sideways glances that they were playing their games with one eye on him and one ear open for the singers. The pitying looks on their faces only made him feel worse.

Eventually, he went to sit on a stone by the school pond and put his head in his hands. He saw a frog peeping at him through the slime but felt so miserable that it wouldn't make much difference if it crawled all over him. After about a dozen renderings of the song were, apparently, ignored by him, the enthusiasm of the singers seemed to flag. There was a lull and a hurried consultation on the wall behind him, then he heard Alex's voice.

"Right, we shall now sing 'Martin a la Carte' to the tune of 'Frère Jacques, frère Jacques, Dormez-vous, dormez-vous'."

David stood up and much to their delight walked around scowling fiercely at them as they sang. Not content with hurting him, they were now poking fun at the sad fate awaiting Martin, his friend. He started picking up stones but then dropped them, knowing that he would only get into more trouble.

Becky at last approached him, looking red in the face. "If you can't do something about it, I shall," she declared. "You can't possibly put up with this for a moment longer."

"What can I do?" he asked helplessly. "My form tutor knows they're picking on me but I can't expect him to hover over my head like a guardian angel all through the lunch hour."

"We'll just have to take one of them to the headmaster to show him what's going on," Becky said determinedly. "When I give the word we'll catch hold of Alex – he's the ringleader – and drag him to the headmaster's study."

David followed as Becky wandered casually over to where they were singing. As the noise reached a crescendo, Becky shouted 'Now!' and suddenly the two of them rushed forward and caught hold of Alex, dragging him down from the wall. Before the others knew what was happening, they pulled him between them, kicking and struggling, along to the headmaster's study. Becky knocked, then pushed the door open and between them they hauled in Alex by the scruff of the neck and the seat of his trousers.

The headmaster was halfway through his lunch and stood up angrily, knife and fork in hand. "What is the meaning of this?" he demanded.

"You tell him, Alex, how you've been picking on David!" Becky cried, "calling him names and singing that horrible song about him."

"What have you been up to again, Edwards?" the headmaster asked. "Hardly a week goes by without someone complaining about you."

“We were just singing a song, sir, and having a bit of fun,” Alex said.

“Tell him the words,” Becky commanded.

“Yes let’s hear them,” the headmaster said sternly, putting down his cutlery. He listened with a worried expression on his face and David cringed as the well-known words of the song were reluctantly repeated by Alex.

“We’ll have to get your parents in on this,” the headmaster said. “I can’t tolerate such behaviour at my school. But I tell you now, David and Becky, that in future you can’t possibly take the law into your own hands in this manner. You should report such bullying to your form tutor and he’ll bring it to my attention in due course. You two can go now, but Alex will stay behind.”

“Sorry, sir, and thank you,” Becky said.

David followed her out quietly, not knowing how much better off he would be because of their militant action.

CHAPTER 16

A tense silence set in after the headmaster had summoned the boys' parents to school and spoken to them. There were no more open taunts and they did not sing their song in public to annoy David. They were ominously quiet as they rode past him on the way home in the evening but his back still twitched when he heard the whirring of their bikes coming up behind him. They deliberately ignored him and this shut him out more completely than their former hostility. He felt sure that something was going on and he had to find out what they were planning to do.

Their 'headquarters' in the evenings was a bench in the park near the chute. David had noticed, when he walked past on his way to the piano lessons, that long grass and trees were located close to the bench on which they sat and he wanted to take a closer look. He knew they'd be up at the rugby field on that Saturday afternoon, watching the match between Croesdy and the neighbouring village of Pantyffynnon, so he decided to visit the park to study the situation. As he expected, there were only girls from the nearby council estate playing on the swings and roundabout at that time of day. He sat on the bench favoured by the boys, feeling a strange thrill running through him at his closeness to them.

He went round behind the bench and tried forcing his way into the nearby rhododendron bushes. Nettles and brambles blocked his path the further he went, so he retreated, knowing that his parents would be annoyed if he returned home with his clothes torn. Then, a few yards away, he noticed a dead tree trunk lying in the deep grass with its base protruding into the bushes. Carefully balancing on top of it, he walked above the undergrowth till he could descend into the cool twilight beyond.

He found himself in a small clearing, an ideal hide-out for listening to their conversations since he was perfectly concealed by the bushes and within hearing distance of the bench. But how was he going to get there without being observed? Wielding a dead branch, he started cutting his way through the undergrowth towards the council estate behind the park, making a tunnel in and out between the trees. At last, he could see light breaking through in front of him and he cautiously emerged into a cul-de-sac on the outskirts of the houses. David decided it was a quiet enough entrance to his secret path and so he retraced his steps till he was once more in his hide-out. He gathered dead leaves together till he had formed a cushion on which he could kneel. Here he could comfortably listen to what they had to say about him.

David retreated through the tunnel, well pleased with his plan, and this time, as he emerged from his secret entrance, he carefully closed the opening behind him with branches. As he straightened and turned, he saw Mandy and Anna playing hopscotch lower down the street. Mandy had stopped in the middle of the game, one leg poised in the air but when he looked at her she continued her jumping from one square to another. Mandy was saying something to Anna, who didn't seem to take much notice of him.

*

After tea on Monday evening, David watched from an upstairs window as Alex, Stan and Aeron cycled past his house on their way to the park. He allowed another half hour for them to settle down to their discussions, then walked round the backs of the council houses. The alley appeared to be deserted as he looked up and down, though he seemed to hear the noise of a smothered laugh. He was imagining things he told himself as he parted the bushes and gained entry to his secret path. David made his way stealthily between the trees, brushing aside the creepers clinging to his hair and being careful not to step on a dry twig. He could hear the murmur of voices gradually becoming audible as he approached the final line of bushes, so he got down on his hands and knees and crawled the last few yards till he was kneeling on a cushion of dead leaves.

As David peered through the branches, he was so close to them that it was like watching a film on the television at home. They were talking about a Beatles concert and David started feeling drowsy then, all at once, his ears pricked up.

"What shall we do about problem child?" Alex asked. "He's the one who got us into this mess."

"We'd better leave him alone now that the Head and our parents are on to us," Aeron said.

"That's nonsense," Alex replied. "We'll have to be sly but we can still get at him."

"We can't let him get away with it," Stan agreed. "We've got to teach him a lesson he'll never forget, and we need to get our own back on that flipping Becky."

"Gwynfor can help us there," Alex said. "He's my cousin and he's told me he's only playing around with her, just having some fun. I've given him one or two ideas."

"Let's get back to problem child," Stan said. "Now that he's afraid of coming down to the river in the evening, he spends a lot of his time on that ledge beneath Cwmfferws bridge. It's quite a drop down to those stones."

"If you leaned over the side you might accidentally bump into him," Alex said.

"He'd have quite a job climbing out of that pool."

"We'll look there every night from now on till we catch him on that ledge," Stan said. "He has to go somewhere in the evenings, he can't just moon about with his goose, and he won't have him after Christmas."

David felt hot and bothered, too ill almost to move but at last he managed to turn and crawl back through the tunnel, with their voices fading behind him like the buzzing of wasps. Mandy and Anna were still playing hopscotch when he emerged from the tunnel and this time they both stopped in mid-stride when they saw him but he blundered out regardless and almost ran home.

That night, as he tossed and turned in his sleep, he dreamt that he was on the ledge beneath Cwmfferws bridge. Suddenly, he saw Alex's face above him and felt Stan's hand on his shoulder.

"No, no!" he screamed, bracing himself against the fall through the air, trying to save himself from breaking his back on the stones.

"What is it, David?" his mother asked, as she hurried into his room. "Have those horrible boys been after you again?"

"I heard some people talking and I can't get what they said out of my mind," he replied, as he turned away from her and hid his face in the pillows.

*

Martin was David's sole companion after school and he'd take him out to the garden even if it was raining. As the evenings darkened earlier in December, he treasured every moment of daylight as he followed Martin's white form around the garden in the gathering gloom. His mother would be calling him to come in, for his food was getting cold and his father was becoming irritable.

"Coming, Mam!" David would call as he gathered Martin up in his arms and held his wings tightly closed as he lowered him into the barrel.

*

A stony silence greeted him at school but the word 'snitcher' was often murmured loudly enough for him to hear. Even boys who used to talk to him now looked away in embarrassment when he tried to join them. Becky was his main companion, which didn't please her friend Mandy when she wanted to have her heart-to-heart, 'girls only' talk with her.

It was lunchtime on that December Friday and Mandy was waiting for Becky to come out of the toilet. David was also hanging around, hoping to have her company.

Mandy came over to stand beside him. "I haven't seen you coming out from your secret path for some time now, David," she said in a surprisingly friendly manner.

"No, the weather is getting too bad for visiting hide-outs," David replied, feeling rather self-conscious. "Water drips from the trees and you get soaking wet in the den."

"I know what you mean, I only go to the park on Sundays in winter. It's not worth bothering in the evenings but the boys are having a special get-together up there this Sunday afternoon – the last of the season you might say – so some of us girls may drop in. Ah, here comes Becky. We've got something very personal to talk about, a woman's little problem you know, David, so if you'll excuse us…"

"Are you all right, David?" Becky asked anxiously.

"David is fine," Mandy assured her. "We've been talking about hide-outs and the two of us may be visiting a den before long."

With that she was off, taking Becky with her. Alex seemed to give her an approving look as they walked past. David felt uneasy, he was so accustomed to Mandy's hostility that her sudden friendliness was scary. He followed some boys to the toilet because it was something to do and he stared at the dark, cracked wall then wandered uncertainly back to the yard. A football match was going on and he strolled a few times around the perimeter without being asked to join in. He looked at his watch and saw that there was still another quarter of an hour to go before Registration.

David drifted back to the classroom, thinking that he might sit in the reader's corner till the bell went. He hesitated on hearing a low whistle as he entered the building, but then carried on. As he was about to open the classroom door, he heard raised voices. He stood there, his hand on the latch, his ears burning as he realised that they were talking about him.

"We'll have to decide this Sunday what we are going to do about problem child," Alex was saying.

"I'm not sure if I can make it this Sunday because I've promised to help on the farm," Aeron replied.

"You'd better be there," Alex snapped. "You've been making too many excuses lately for not joining us. You're either with us or against us."

"I can get there by three on Sunday afternoon," Stan volunteered.

"Three it will have to be then," Alex said. "Anna can put on some light entertainment to get us in the right mood and we'll have our meeting after."

"Let's hope she shows us a bit more than she did last time," Stan said sulkily. "We're not there to admire her skill as a dancer. We gave her sweets and fags last time and she didn't even take her top off."

"I'll talk to her first," Alex promised. "I've got a way with girls."

David heard footsteps coming along the corridor and quickly made his way out to the yard. He walked round and round the perimeter of the football match till the bell rang and then sat at his solitary desk for Registration.

*

As he came out of school at the end of the afternoon, Becky was waiting for him.

"I thought you'd be meeting Gwynfor at the bus stop," he said uncertainly.

"He gets off his bus a stop earlier these days to avoid seeing me," Becky said bitterly. "He doesn't want anything to do with me now I've laid down the rules."

"Perhaps you could have a chat with Mandy if it's a girl's problem that's bothering you," David suggested, feeling rather embarrassed.

"Everybody would hear about it if I told her," Becky said, "and I don't want Gwynfor to find out that I've been talking about him. No, David, you're the only one I can trust. Let's go to the rugby ground."

"I can't be long," David said, as he followed Becky down the road. "I've got to take Martin for a walk and clean out his barrel before it gets dark."

After that they walked in silence till they came to a deserted corner of the rugby field. Becky turned to face him with tears in her eyes.

"Gwynfor has finished with me," she said, "and I've felt miserable ever since."

"Will you try to make it up with him?" David asked uncertainly.

Becky brushed away a tear. "I don't know what I'm going to do," she replied. "Dad doesn't want to see Gwynfor anywhere near me but he's my first love."

David put his arm around her shoulders and tried to comfort her though he didn't know what to say. Suddenly she broke away.

"Thank you for trying to help me, David, but it's no good. Gwynfor is the only one I want with me now," she muttered, and with that she turned and half walked, half ran on her journey home.

*

David and his father heard the letter box clamping that Saturday morning and there on the mat by the front door lay a letter addressed to Mrs Blink.

"It must be the wrong address," his father said puzzled as he picked it up, "there's no Mrs Blink living here. Let's see, 14 Hafod Road, Croesdy, but that's us. I haven't heard of the surname 'Blink' before, have you, David?"

"Perhaps it's someone Mam knows," David said.

"Yes, yes, she'll know how to sort it out. Just put it with her things over there."

David did as he was told and then went upstairs to carry on with his English short story but he couldn't concentrate and his mind kept returning to that letter. Who was addressing his mother as Mrs Blink and what did they have to tell her? Was this a letter about him, the so-called 'Dai Blink'?

David tried to focus again on his crime fiction story. How would Gari Tryfan, his favourite detective, deal with this kind of harassment? He would work out who was responsible by a process of logical deduction but that wasn't David's problem. He knew full well who had written the letter but how could he stop the bullies from threatening his family life?

David heard his father stomping about in his boots as he prepared to go up to the old colliery for his Saturday afternoon walk. He'd be wandering around on the grassed-over tips thinking about how he used to work as a boy in the deserted tunnels beneath his feet. David heard the door closing behind his father and then he couldn't restrain himself from fetching the envelope propped up on his mother's sideboard. He put the kettle on to boil and held the seal in the steam till it softened and he could risk levering up the flap. As was to be expected, there was no address and the letter consisted of seven lines printed to disguise the handwriting.

Dear Mrs Blink,

I have to inform you that your son David does not have long to live unless he changes his ways and becomes one of the boys instead of toadying up to the teachers. He has made himself very unpopular with all of us and deserves the fate worse than death which awaits him. You also are at fault in making him think that he is better than the rest of us. We advise you to make arrangements beforehand with Sam James, the undertaker, so that your son can have a reasonably priced funeral.

Yours faithfully,

One who has your best interests at heart.

David strode up and down the room feeling very angry at first. How dare those bullies try to upset his parents? His first reaction was to write a similar letter addressed to Alex's mother saying that her son was going to be hunted down and harpooned like a whale. Then he thought of how they'd publicize his letter in the neighbourhood and leave people in no doubt as to who was the author. They might even call in the police and such a letter could rebound on David, getting him into worse trouble. His parents couldn't live with such a scandal, so he had to employ more discreet methods.

In his increasing agitation, David considered the likely effects of the letter. It was upsetting enough for him but it would make his mother worry herself sick. He couldn't possibly allow her to read it but his father was bound to say that a strange letter had arrived addressed to Mrs Blink. All he could do was compose something relatively innocuous to put in its place. He returned to the table and pushing his homework aside, he set about composing his first anonymous letter, taking care to print the letters so that his mother wouldn't recognise his handwriting. He wrote:

> Dear Mrs Blink,
> It has been brought to our attention that your son David has unfortunately acquired a nickname. We hope that you won't be unduly distressed by the nickname 'Blink' because it is, after all, a reflection of his academic tendency to read for long hours. Please be patient with boys who call him by that name for they are only jealous of his excellence at school.
> Yours faithfully,
> A blinking sympathiser.

David carefully folded the letter, inserted it in the envelope and re-sealed it with a glue stick before returning it to his mother's sideboard. He was then able to re-immerse himself in his homework and was busy writing when his mother came up to his room later that evening.

"I met your father on my way home," she said. "He told me that a strange letter addressed to a Mrs Blink had arrived."

"Yes, Mam," David said, as casually as he could, "we left it on the sideboard for you."

He followed his mother downstairs and watched as she tore open the envelope and then read the contents. "How strange," she muttered.

"What is it, Mam?" David asked.

"Oh it's nothing much, dear," his mother replied as she hurriedly put it in her handbag. "It's a letter from someone who affectionately addresses me as Mrs Blink. It's a person whom I haven't seen for a long time." Her eyes were bright as she set about preparing supper.

CHAPTER 17

David walked with his parents to chapel that Sunday morning. The decorations in the High Street windows reminded him that Christmas was only twelve days away.

Mr Mathews, the minister, was standing by the door to welcome the members of his congregation as they arrived.

"The joy of the season be with you," he said.

The Sunday school pupils went forward to recite their verses from the Bible.

David's mother had wanted him to learn a verse from the Christmas story but David preferred to say an old favourite.

"One generation comes and another passes away but the earth endures for ever. The sun also shines upon the godly and the ungodly," he said solemnly. He returned to his seat and tried to find comfort in the words of the sermon.

"Christ has promised that He will be with us till the end of the world and it is in this knowledge, brothers and sisters, that we move forward," Mr Mathews assured them. "After His suffering on the cross, he will be with us forever in our hearts."

David changed quickly from his Sunday suit after returning home and went out to fetch Martin from the shed. He had become so heavy by now that David could hardly lift him out of the barrel. Martin rubbed gratefully against his legs and was then off, stomping across the garden, plunging his beak in knowingly, here and there, and wrenching out a rare worm. When he got to the bath, he managed to haul himself onto the rim by a combination of jumps and flaps. As he flopped in, the water overflowed all around him but Martin joyously swam round and round his narrowing circle. David watched him enraptured until a waspish voice came over the hedge.

David had a little goose
He ate it with orange sauce
And wherever David went
The little goose went too.

He looked round to see Alex and Stan balancing against the hedge on their bikes.

"He's having his final run around, is he?" Stan asked, but David said nothing.

Aeron had by now joined them but seemed disinclined to enter into the mood of the other two as he rode round and round on the outskirts.

"It can't be long now before Martin's great day, can it?" Alex asked. "It'll have to be a few days before

Christmas so they can hang him up for the meat to set. Please let us know when they're killing him, Dai; I wouldn't miss it for the world."

"Why don't you just mind your own business and push off!" David shouted, his fingers trembling as he leant on the bath.

Alex and Stan laughed delightedly but Aeron gave David a sympathetic look as they rode away.

"I'd better take you back to your house," David said, as he went over and hauled Martin out of the bath. Water cascaded off his wings as he shook himself. He squawked in protest all the way back to the shed and gave David a reproving look as he was squeezed into his barrel. Then he thrust his beak down into his feathers and lay there sulking.

"It's for your own good, you're safer in there," David told him, as he replaced the netting wire over the top.

He walked around restlessly, not knowing what to do with himself. Then he remembered what he had overheard outside the classroom; they were meeting in the park to talk about him that afternoon. His hiding place was ready; he'd have to be there to know what they intended doing.

Lunch passed in a daze, and so he walked around the garden aimlessly afterwards for he was afraid of letting Martin out. Then it was time for him to go to the park. As he approached, he saw that Mandy was skipping in the cul-de-sac by the council estate but she disappeared as he was about to enter his secret path. All seemed quiet as he looked up and down the deserted street before squeezing in between the brambles and closing the branches behind him. David made his way through the decaying undergrowth and in and out among the trees. He heard voices getting louder in front of him as he crawled the last few yards over the fallen leaves to his hide-out beneath the bushes. If he stood up, he'd be face to face with Alex and Aeron who were talking loudly.

Where was Stan he asked himself, but he couldn't look round as he was now stuck in his crouched position. The boys were soon joined by Anna and after they had reluctantly parted with some cigarettes and sweets she turned up the music on her Walkman and started dancing. Was there a rustling in the undergrowth behind him David asked himself uneasily as he settled down to wait, knowing that the boys were unlikely to start any serious discussion till Stan arrived. Anna had taken off her jumper and was warming up to her dancing. Suddenly, she was joined by Mandy, who whispered something in her ear, and then the two of them threw themselves into a frenzied dance.

David heard a muffled thud in the trees behind him but assumed it was a rabbit or a bird as he was well accustomed to such noises when he went fishing. Mandy and Anna took off their T-shirts and waved them in the air as they reached the climax of their dance. Alex and Aeron gave appreciative wolf whistles as Anna gave a final twirl and then held up her hand for silence.

"Thank you for showing your appreciation of our dancing skills," she said. "Now, I've been told by my friend Mandy that we have a VIP in our presence this afternoon, a great scholar at the Croesdy Academy who knows the meaning of 'fait accompli'!"

Alex turned to smile in his direction and then to his horror it dawned on David that she was talking about him and they knew that he was there. He began back-pedalling on his knees through the undergrowth but soon came up against something hard and unyielding behind him. Looking down, he saw the black toe-cap of Stan's boot between his knees and felt his shoulders gripped by Stan's rough hands. He tried to struggle free but then felt a stinging pain as his hair was pulled.

"You stay still, Dai Blink, or I'll pull out every hair by its roots!" Stan warned him. "Those who listen to other people's conversations don't hear any good of themselves. Get up on your feet, mun, or I'll have to drag you along like a pig to the bench."

David stood up painfully. He blundered forward through the brambles tearing his clothes, with Stan pushing him from behind, till he came face to face with Alex sitting on the base of the chute.

*

It was getting dark early that Sunday afternoon. Grey lowering clouds were devouring the last of the December sunshine and cars passing to and fro behind the trees had already turned on their headlights.

"What is David doing out on such a dismal afternoon?" his mother asked anxiously as she peered out of the kitchen window at the greyness outside. "It's only a quarter past four but it's already getting dark."

"He's probably playing football with his pals up at the park," his father replied optimistically. "You know what boys are like, they'll be kicking the ball around till they can hardly see it."

"I know he's got homework to do by tomorrow," his mother continued, "and it's not like him to leave it till the last minute."

"It's nice to see him going out for a change," his father said, as he returned to reading the Sunday newspaper. "He's too often at home, if you ask me, moping over his books. It'll do him good to get some fresh air."

*

David was getting more than his share of fresh air in the park that Sunday afternoon as Alex drove him up the chute.

"Up you go," Alex urged, jabbing a stick once more into his behind.

David's feet ascended one metal rung at a time as he

was forced up the chute. He tried not to look down as the height made him dizzy. At last, he reached the small metal platform at the top and gripped the railing.

"Right, down you go, head first," Alex commanded hoarsely from behind.

David bent forward like a diver, his arms extended in front of him. He lowered his chest towards the cold metal, trying to brace himself against the sides to make his descent as slow as possible. They had been polishing the chute and he knew that the moment he let go he'd go hurtling down, head first.

He couldn't bring himself to loosen his fingers. He straightened and balanced, head up in the cold air. He looked down at Aeron, Mandy and Anna gathered together at the foot of the chute while Alex and Stan stood behind him on the metal rungs, urging him on.

"Go on, you eavesdropper!" Alex shouted, as he goaded him on. "You know now what we think of you!"

"You've got to take your punishment like a man!" Stan exclaimed.

The darkening playground all around was deserted as the children playing there earlier had all gone home, not wanting to be involved, but Aeron was still there, standing ashamedly at the foot of the chute while Mandy and Anna were unusually quiet.

David looked at the shining chute once again and then at the concrete down on his right. Was there any escape from these tormentors who were making his life a misery? He was suddenly numb to the pain gnawing at the bottom of his stomach as he began to feel giddy and started swaying.

"No!" Aeron shouted, and then he was scrambling desperately up the chute towards him, sliding with every step he took, hauling himself up hand over hand on the rims on each side. David was trembling on the metal platform but Aeron reached him just in time and caught hold of him in his strong arms.

"We're going back down the steps together," Aeron said, as he turned him round gently but firmly.

He saw Alex beneath him, holding the stick uncertainly in his hand and Stan, looking puzzled for once.

"Out of the way, you maniacs, unless you want to be locked up!" Aeron said impatiently, as he guided David down, step by step.

"You're not letting him go," Alex protested, but one look from Aeron was enough to make him drop the stick and clamber down in front of them.

"We're taking him home," Aeron told Stan, "give me a hand."

"But we can't let him get away with it, not after going to all this trouble," Alex protested, as he tried to block their path. "We'll wait for him to recover then take him back up the chute."

"Do you want us to be had up for murder?" Aeron

asked angrily, as he shoved him aside. He and Stan supported David with their arms under his shoulders as he collapsed between them.

"We're taking you home on condition that we won't hear anything more about this business," Alex insisted, as the other two helped him along. "Promise us, Dai, that you won't tell any one."

"I promise," David mumbled, ready to say anything to bring the nightmare to an end.

His parents were visiting their next door neighbour when the boys left him at the door. David managed to open it, then he stumbled upstairs and fell on his bed.

CHAPTER 18

Monday passed in a daze for David after the episode on the chute. Nothing was said to him at school by the others and their eyes avoided his. A space seemed to open around him out in the yard. They were waiting for him to make his move and he felt almost in control of the situation. He was glad that he had made the effort to go to school and face them, though his mother had begged him to stay at home that morning because he looked so ill. It had been his day, he reflected, as he came out at the end of the afternoon session and noted with some satisfaction that they had already pushed off on their bikes. It was then that he heard Mandy and Anna giggling behind him and painfully realised that they were making fun of him.

"What are you two up to?" he demanded.

"We'd like to ask you a few questions," Anna said.

"Right, be quick about it as I'm on my way home," he replied.

"Did you enjoy watching us dance and did you like what you saw?" Mandy asked slyly.

"Would you like to go out with one of us?" Anna asked enticingly.

"Seeing you twirling around in your bras is not my idea of entertainment and I get enough of your company at school," David answered. "I don't think I'd want to spend an extra half hour with either of you behind the changing rooms!"

Mandy scowled. "Right, there's just one more question. What was that funny smell when you were stuck on top of the chute?"

David turned crimson as the girls burst out laughing and ran past him out through the school gates. He stood there feeling humiliated and then anger seemed to take over. They had made a fool of him yet again but they were not getting away with it this time. He would find a way of getting his revenge.

David walked home in a temper and then, as he was rounding the square, he happened to glance down the alley at the side of the hardware shop. He caught a glimpse of the familiar rear wheels of his tormentors' bikes parked beside the oil-stores behind the shop. He was about to hurry on but the cold anger building up inside him made him pause, then look up and down before venturing down the alley to investigate. The three of them had gone into the oil-stores, pulling the door shut behind them. He could see Alex inside with his back to the barred window, sitting on a paraffin drum while the other two were perched on oil barrels.

David flinched as Alex half-turned to tap his

cigarette on the window sill and almost looked at him. David stooped hurriedly beneath the window and then crept round to listen by the door. At first he could only hear an indistinct murmur but then he began putting together the threatening words.

"We're safe," he heard Alex say, "he's too afraid… won't tell anybody… bide our time… another go at him later."

"… safer to leave him alone…" Stan said. "… he's had a fright… top of that chute… real trouble… opens his mouth."

"I'm opening this window to let in some fresh air," Aeron said as he impatiently thrust open the small narrow window which almost brushed the top of David's head. "It's time you blokes realised how close we came to disaster. Just think of the position we'd be in if he'd fallen from the top of the chute. We'd be locked up in jail by now."

"I'd have found a way out for us," Alex assured him. "We'd have claimed that he was playing about on the chute when he got stuck and we were trying to help him come down safely. No, he still thinks he's better than us, that's his trouble, and we can't let him get away with it. We've got to hurt him more and still more till he gives in."

Trembling with rage, David looked at the metal bar on the outside of the door. He thought of the inconvenience to them if he locked them in. They'd be shouting and banging for ages before anyone came to answer and then they'd get a telling off from Jenkins the Oil for playing about in his shed. David crept up to the door and gripped the bar with his hand, its coldness seemed to burn into his skin as he lowered it quietly into position across the door, but then he paused. Was getting them told off enough of a revenge or should he go further? What if a fire broke out in the shed while they were smoking and the bar was then lowered with them inside? His moment had not yet come. Quietly, he raised the bar and made his way out of the yard.

As he rounded the corner, he saw Jenkins approaching, ready to lock up.

"Ah, Mr Jenkins," he said, raising his voice so the boys could hear him through the open window of the shed. "I see you're about to shut shop but my parents sent me to buy a box of matches." He felt in his pocket and found to his relief that he had enough money.

"Just when I was about to close," Jenkins grumbled. "Oh well, you'd better come in, your parents are good customers of mine."

As he paid for the matches, David was pleased to see the boys riding past on their bikes. He didn't want them to be trapped in the shed, not just yet.

*

David had just crossed off another school day on his calendar, there were only two left now before his longed-for holiday, when there was a knock on the door. It was Dewi on his way home from work, leaning his burly frame against the doorstep.

"I called with your uncle – thought he might want a hand with the goose tonight – but he's not around."

David felt faint but forced himself to speak calmly. "No, he wouldn't be, he goes early to the Bingo down in Llanelli on Monday night and comes home late."

"Oh well, we'll have to delay it then," Dewi said.

"Can I take a message?" David asked.

"Yes, tell him I'll be calling this time tomorrow night. We'll have to do it then so the goose can hang for a few days. It'll give flavour to the meat."

"I'll let him know," was all David could manage to say.

"Who was that?" his mother asked.

"One of Uncle Myrdd's friends wanted a word with him," David replied.

He went to the shed and lifted Martin out of the barrel. "This is your last run round," he said sadly, as he watched him scrabbling in the garden though the soil was hard and worms were lying deep since the first frost.

He followed Martin as he made his way over to the bath, then broke the thin sheet of ice and helped him scramble into the water. Rather you than me, David thought, as he felt the bitterly cold water clasping his fingers.

Martin squeezed his way round the bath though his feet were by now touching the bottom and he couldn't paddle properly.

"I'd have had to get you a larger bath, anyway," David said regretfully.

"It doesn't matter, Master," Martin mimicked out of the corner of his mouth. "This will do for the time being."

David looked across the darkening fields behind the house to the Cae Helyg woods in the distance. It was there the local fox lay in wait for any stray poultry.

Yet Martin would stand a better chance with the fox than against the combined forces of Uncle Myrdd and Dewi. David looked thoughtfully at a former gap in the hedge, which his father had patched up with dead brambles. He went over in the gathering dusk and dragged out dead sticks till there was room for Martin to squeeze his way through.

"Tea is ready!" his mother called.

"Coming Mother," David said. "I'll just put Martin away for the night."

Martin got up on the rim of the bath as he saw David approaching and gave him the usual welcoming shower. David half carried him to his escape route and then encouraged him to push his way through.

Martin squawked in surprise and half turned when he reached the field, looking lost, as if expecting David to fetch him back in.

"You're on your own now," David said firmly, as he thrust the dead sticks back into place to close the gap between them.

Martin squawked again, raising his great wings in alarm but then the novelty of having the fields in front of him took his attention and he was off. David saw his pale shape becoming fainter as he headed in the direction of the Cae Helyg woods.

"Are you coming in for your food or shall I fetch you, boy!" shouted his exasperated father.

"Coming Dad," he replied, banging the shed door on his way back to the house.

There was an uneasy silence as he ate his meal.

"I thought Myrdd and Dai would be calling round to see about the goose tonight," his father said presently.

His mother looked anxiously at David. "Surely not," she said, "it's Myrdd's night out at the Bingo and I can't see him giving that up for anybody. Besides, there's another six days before Christmas."

"Poultry should be hung for a few days to give it relish and it's the right weather for that just now," his father said, stretching his feet out to the fire.

"I'll have to go upstairs to draw maps for my Geography homework," David said presently.

He just couldn't bear to sit down and talk to his

parents in his excited state of mind. His thoughts were with Martin in the Cae Helyg woods as he tried to concentrate on his homework; he imagined the fox picking up his scent and closing in on him. David hurriedly turned to the book *Wild Creatures in British Habitats*, which he had borrowed that day from the school library. He looked up the section on the hunting habits of foxes and was relieved to read that a fox seldom attacked a creature bigger than itself. A comforting picture came to him of Martin towering above the fox, flapping his great wings and stabbing at it with his beak till the fox retreated.

But how was Martin going to feed himself in the wild, especially now that the earth was hard with frost? David couldn't bear to think of Martin starving to death then he remembered how Pip used to smuggle food to Magwitch in *Great Expectations*. He'd have to prepare a bagful of scraps last thing at night ready to take across the fields to Martin after school. Pretending that he was still hungry, he went downstairs to the kitchen and half filled an empty ice-cream container with leftovers which he then hid in his school bag.

His next problem was how to explain the disappearance of Martin to his uncle and Dai when they came the following evening. David remembered how his uncle had a great respect for the cunning of the local fox and thought that he might be able to play on that. He recalled how his uncle had held the fox responsible for the disappearance of a pet rabbit from its hutch a few years previously. His mother had hinted darkly that it was a fox with two legs that had taken the rabbit, but this had failed to convince his uncle. David would have to confess to not shutting the shed door properly but he was prepared to take the blame for being absent-minded.

By eight o'clock he was in better spirits now that he was making an effort to save Martin. Then there was a knock on the door and David assumed that it was a relative delivering a Christmas card or a present, but then his father called him.

He went to the door and to his surprise, he saw Aeron standing there.

"I've been out 'lamping' with my brother Arwel," he said, "and we thought you might like to come out to the van to see the rabbits we've caught."

David was about to refuse indignantly because he strongly disapproved of the sport which they called 'lamping'. A rabbit would be dazzled by a powerful beam of light and then the dogs were released to catch it.

"We've been 'lamping' in the Cae Helyg woods," Aeron repeated, winking slyly.

Something clicked in David's mind and he nodded in agreement. "I'll be back now, Dad," he said.

"Take your time," his father said tolerantly. "I used

to enjoy going after rabbits with a ferret and net when I was your age."

His mother came to the door with a worried expression. "But David has got homework to do," she said sharply.

"Tut, tut, woman," his father said. "Boys will be boys and they want to show off to each other when they've caught something. I spent some of the happiest days of my life ferreting and it did me no harm."

"I've got a little present for you out here," Aeron said as David followed him to the van. Arwel, his elder brother, opened the rear door and switched on his torch.

In the beam of light, David could see Martin cowering in the corner, his bill in his feathers. Bloodstained rabbits lay around his feet.

"You're lucky the other poachers didn't get to him first or he'd have lead pellets in him by now," Arwel said. "And believe you me, a knife is much kinder than that."

"Was he all right when you saw him?" David asked.

"I think the fox must have frightened him for Martin came to me at once when I called his name," Aeron said. "He may have remembered who gave him that plastic duck."

"Thanks for saving him," David said brokenly.

"I wanted to make up to you for what happened on the chute," Aeron said. "I'll help you take him quietly round to the shed to save you getting into trouble."

"I'll manage on my own," David replied. He picked up the cowed Martin and with the other two watching, he staggered with him in his arms to the temporary safety of the shed. Breathlessly, he lowered him into his barrel for the last time. Martin squawked and looked up at him gratefully and David mimicked him saying, "Thank you, kind master, for trying to save me."

CHAPTER 19

The classroom was decorated for the last day of the Christmas term and most of the pupils were giving each other cards and presents. David sat on his own, pretending to read a magazine but when he saw his chance he presented Becky with a card and a small box of chocolates. She gave him a tearful smile and handed him a card and some sweets.

This little exchange was seen by Stan, who brought it to Alex's attention. "You watch it, Dai, or you'll be making Gwynfor jealous," Alex whispered, taking care not to let Becky hear him. "But then again, perhaps she's desperate enough now to go with you. I wonder why?"

Becky turned suddenly as if she had guessed what Alex said. "Well at least I haven't stooped low enough to pay attention to you, Alex!" she snapped, stamping suddenly on the floor so that he retreated hurriedly. "I think that having one of you around is more than enough!"

"My cousin will make you pay for this," he snarled, trying not to lose face.

Becky suddenly went very quiet and buried her face in her hands but Alex lacked the courage to drive home his advantage.

David felt obliged to tag on to Becky in the lunch hour in case he could help her but Mandy soon joined them and wasn't keen on having David around.

"Can't you see when you're not wanted?" she snapped. "We've got girly things to talk about and you'd better wear a skirt if you want to join in."

David could see that Becky was almost crying and in no condition to stand up to Mandy.

"I just wanted to know if she was all right," he said defensively.

"She'll be safer with me than with you or any other boy," Mandy said dismissively. "Now buzz off if you know what's good for you."

David walked round and round the yard by himself. Suddenly Alex and Stan, followed reluctantly by Aeron, were closing in upon him.

"If you've got a moment to spare," Alex said, "we'd like to give you a little Christmas present."

"Something to remind you of the good times we've had together this term and a little taster of what you can look forward to this evening," Stan said.

"Here you are," Alex said, placing a brown paper parcel in his hands, "and as a token of Christmas goodwill we'd like you to open it in our presence."

David didn't know what to think and he glanced at Aeron, who avoided his eyes, looking distinctly uncomfortable. By now, a little group had gathered round and there was an air of anticipation as David fumbled with the parcel.

Slowly he opened it, noting to his horror that the inner layer of brown paper was blood stained and, as he opened it right out, a cockerel's head flanked by its feet looked up at him with one glazed, bloodshot eye seeming to glare into his. He tried to throw away the parcel but it stuck to his nerveless hands.

"And that's how your goose will end up tonight," Alex said.

With that, Stan suddenly knocked up David's hands so that the cockerel's head and feet came flying up into his face and he and Alex ran away laughing. David stood there, looking at the head lying on the floor, imagining that it was Martin staring up at him in a few hours time.

Aeron came to stand beside him for a few moments. "Sorry about that, Dave," he said. Ashamedly, he picked up the head and feet and put them in a bin.

The boys shot past David on their bikes on the way home from school as if they had something in mind. David lagged behind the others and thought of going for a long walk. How could he face going home to see Martin being killed? Anything was better than that, so he turned his steps towards the park almost hoping that visiting the scene of his torment again would put Martin out of his mind. The swings and the chute were deserted on that frosty evening, but as he approached them he saw the bushes moving in his former hide-out. He walked over uncertainly but suddenly Mandy and Gwynfor stood up facing him.

"I always knew you were a peeping Tom, Dai Blink," Mandy said scornfully as she smoothed down her school uniform.

"Go away, you creep," Gwynfor said angrily, "and remember, you haven't seen anything or I'll put Alex on to you."

"May I remind you, Gwynfor, that you're not in a position to call anyone a creep," David said, as he bravely chose his words, "and I thought you, Mandy, would be getting used to peeping Toms by now but I don't have any sweets to give you."

He turned away, ignoring the angry shouts of 'Dai Blink' behind him and walked over to the rugby field, intending to run round and round the perimeter till he was too tired to worry about what his uncle and Dewi had done to Martin in his absence.

David started running round the touch-lines and dead-ball areas of the deserted pitch and was staggering around on his third lap when he heard someone calling him. He guessed who it was even before he looked up and indeed it was Becky waving to him helplessly from behind the dressing rooms. They could both look forward to having a most unpleasant evening, he thought grimly as he walked over.

"I needn't ask you this time if you've seen Gwynfor," she said. "I asked Mandy to tell him it was his last chance to meet me here tonight but I knew it was no good. In fact, I guessed from that guilty look on her face that she was carrying on with him behind my back."

David just couldn't bear to make her more miserable by telling her what he had seen in the park but he stood close to her and she rested her head on his chest. He put his arm around her shoulders comfortingly and tried to think how horrible it was for a girl to be betrayed by her friend.

"This is going to be the worst Christmas since Mam went away," Becky said.

She stood there clinging to him for five minutes or more till his shirt was wet with her tears. "Thank you, Dave," she said, straightening at last. "I feel strong enough now to go home to face my problems. Are you coming?"

Home was the last place he wanted to visit but when she parted from him at the gate his feet took him round the corner.

"Where have you been, boy?" his father demanded. "I'm expecting Myrdd and Dewi here any minute and your help may be needed to hold the goose."

"Don't you dare mention that again, Isaac!" his mother exclaimed. "David is staying in here with me to watch television. You should know, Isaac, how attached he is to that goose. Come and have your dinner, David, I've kept it warm for you in the oven."

David felt relieved at first when he realised that Martin was still alive but increasingly apprehensive as he knew what was going to happen that evening. He toyed with his food, hoping desperately that his uncle couldn't come. Perhaps there was Bingo on every night in Llanelli that week in the run up to Christmas.

There was a knock on the door and as his father answered he heard Alex's voice. "We've come to see the goose being killed, if that's all right with you, Isaac."

"I don't mind at all, boys, but the men are a bit late arriving. Perhaps you can hold it for me now while I do it myself."

"We're with you there, Mister," Stan replied promptly, "I've often held a pig or a sheep for my father on the farm."

David stopped fiddling with his food and put his head down on his hands.

His mother got up and rushed to the door. "No more of this barbaric nonsense!" she cried. "I don't want any of you lot around. You should be ashamed of yourselves, wanting to see a creature being killed."

David's father stood there awkwardly as the boys retreated. "It's a tradition," he said defensively, "boys have to know how it's done. An animal has to be killed for us to eat."

"Tradition indeed!" his wife stormed. "There are

good and bad traditions and we're supposed to be living in a civilized society. If there's any more of this nonsense, David will be keeping his goose permanently as a pet."

"What about my garden in the spring when the goose pulls everything up?" Isaac demanded, "and he'll need a bigger barrel and bath. This reminds me of those sacred cows in India. 'Mawredd mawr!' We'll end up with just that precious goose here! There won't be any room for the rest of us."

CHAPTER 20

It was almost half past seven when Uncle Myrdd and Dewi arrived. David had been dreading it so much that the knock on the door made him jump. The sound of their voices left him in no doubt and his father came in excitedly to collect his cap and then they were off to the shed. His mother turned up the volume on the television and tried to interest David in *Pobol y Cwm*, the Welsh equivalent of *Coronation Street*, but he hurried up to his room at the back of the house. From there he could look down into the garden and, as he knelt on the carpet by the window with his forehead touching the cold glass, he could hear Martin squawking in alarm. By the noise, David knew he was being dragged out of his barrel and then carried from view round the back of the shed. The moonlight was unusually bright because of the frosty weather and in its light, David saw the men emerging onto the garden path with the pale form of Martin struggling between them; then he saw the boys hurrying after them.

"Hang on, wait for us!" he heard Alex shouting.

"Can we hold a leg each?" Stan asked.

"It's OK by me but don't get in the way," Dewi

warned them, “he’s got powerful wings and might do you an injury.”

The window was misting up but David couldn’t drag himself away from it. They were now grouped in a semicircle around Martin as they held him with his neck distended above the garden ditch. He saw the quick flash of a knife and then Martin was shrieking with pain and trying to beat his powerful wings. One wing broke free and caught Alex a glancing blow on the side of the head which knocked him into the garden. Then Martin seemed to be coughing into the gutter till the noise became fainter and fainter and his wings collapsed around him. The men lifted and shook the crumpled mass of feathers till a final flurry of drops came from him as if he’d been having a bath.

David indistinctly heard Stan saying, “That was great, he had loads of blood in him. Can we please keep the head?”

Alex was in no mood to join in the celebrations as he walked around clutching his sore ear and complaining bitterly.

David stepped away dizzily from the window and lay down on the carpet, covering his head with his hands.

“I wish we’d never seen that goose,” he heard his mother say later that night as his father lifted David’s trembling body and laid him on the bed.

“Getting too fond of an animal doesn’t pay, I learnt

that when I was a boy and the pig in the sty at the top of our garden had to be killed in November," Isaac said. "My father had to remind me that having bacon joints hanging from the ceiling to feed us through the winter was more important than keeping the pig as a pet."

*

The first day of the holidays was bright and sunny but David dreaded going out to the shed. Finally, he made himself open the door and saw before him his friend Martin hanging upside down from the crossbeam. He had been stripped of his feathers and blood dripped into a bucket from the headless stump of his neck.

"I'm sorry I let you down," David said, as he forced himself to go forward to touch the coldness of his skin. It was what his mother had told him to do when his grandmother had died. It had helped him to accept that she was dead.

It was the most miserable Christmas dinner ever.

"Try to eat some," his father urged him.

"Which part of Martin is this?" he asked, as he tried to nibble a small piece of the dark meat.

His mother seemed to have lost much of her usual appetite. "Try eating some of the vegetables," she advised David, "and I'll open a tin of corned beef to go with them."

Neither of his parents argued with him when he got up and left the table. He walked up the garden path. A dribble of feathers and blood could still be seen beside the gutter. Martin's bath was standing by the base of the apple tree, it was half full and the plastic duck was bobbing about in the light breeze. He heard someone coughing behind him and, turning, he saw Aeron leaning his bike against the hedge and looking sympathetically at him.

"I'm sorry you've lost him," Aeron said uncertainly.

David looked at the empty garden without saying a word.

"I'll have the plastic duck back, now you've finished with it. My brother wants to use it as a decoy to attract the wild ducks to our pond."

David didn't answer, he just walked over to the bath, caught hold of the duck and threw it to Aeron.

"Your mates will have more than that back," he added under his breath as Aeron pedalled away.

When he returned to the house, his mother handed him a parcel. "It's for you," she said, "it's been thrust in through the letter box. It seems like a last-minute Christmas present."

David went up to his room to open the parcel, thinking perhaps it was a little something from Becky.

As he undid the string, Martin's bloodstained head fell out. David forced himself to pick it up and looked into the eyes, which were still surprisingly bright. He suddenly felt cold as ice and more composed than he had been for days.

"Whatever you've suffered they will suffer more," he promised the head, "and you'll be there to see it happen."

He carefully re-wrapped the present and placed it on a shelf above the empty barrel in the shed.

His parents were out when Jenkins the Oil called an hour later. "Do you know if it's the usual gallon of paraffin they want?" Jenkins asked.

"I think you'd better make it two gallons this time," David said.

"Yes, indeed, you're wise to stock up in case we have a hard January," Jenkins observed approvingly.

"It's going to be very hard for some," David said.

He remembered how he had hidden his broken fishing rod in the hedge near the square in order to defend himself against a bike attack. He thought of hiding a gallon of paraffin in the same place and pouring it under the door of the oil-store while they were holding a meeting. Suddenly, David felt ashamed of himself for harbouring such nasty thoughts but he hurriedly took the two tins to the shed, and stacked them in the corner behind Martin's barrel.

"I'll have nothing to do with the rage that kills," he told himself firmly. "Teaching them a lesson will have to be enough."

David reached up for the bloodstained parcel on the shelf above and took it down. As he opened it again, he saw that Martin's eyes were no longer bright and alert as in the days when he led him out into the garden. Now they were glazed in death as they looked unseeing into David's eyes. "You won't be there to see the moment of your triumph," David told him, "but you'll live in my memory whenever I walk around our garden. Now I shall find a suitable resting place for you."

He dug a hole between two of his dead fish in the circle of tiny graves surrounding the flower bed, then he laid Martin's head to rest and smoothed down the earth over it.

David was glad to see the Christmas festivities drawing to an end and the New Year celebrations also left him cold. Changing the date on the calendar hadn't solved his problems.

On the last day of the holidays, he called round to see Becky and to wish her a Happy New Year. She looked thin and white as she let him in but was obviously glad of his company. He gave her a little packet of chocolate eclairs and she kissed him lightly on the cheek but she still looked distinctly unhappy.

"What is it, dear?" he asked her protectively.

"After seeing Gwynfor hanging around with Mandy, I felt I'd be glad to get rid of such a creep but now I'm not so sure."

"I suppose it takes time to put someone out of your mind," David said. "Perhaps Gwynfor will disappear from the scene."

"That isn't possible, he'll have to stay on at the Tech to finish his course. No, I'll just have to put up with seeing him with Mandy," Becky said, "but you let me know if you have any more trouble from Alex and his cronies. They can't be allowed to make your life a misery."

"There's no need for you to worry, Becky. I'm getting stronger now and they won't bother me for much longer," David assured her.

He went for a walk after leaving Becky's house. The park was deserted and when he walked over to the chute the railing felt cold like gun metal and his hand seemed glued to it. David looked at the bench where they had sat and the bushes in which he had been trapped; he looked up at the platform where they had made him stand, dizzy and faint. He continued his walk past Tommy's house; he had one more piano examination to pass before his parents bought him a bicycle.

It was getting dark and there was no sign of the boys but David knew where to find them. As he rounded the corner by the hardware shop, he could hear their voices coming from the shed at the back of the yard. As he tiptoed down the alley, he saw the glow of light from an oil lamp which they had lit and placed on the window sill. Aeron was sitting with his back to the window and David could gather from the movements of his shoulders that he was playing cards and smoking with the others. They were so intent on their game that if someone quietly barred the door from outside they wouldn't notice anything. They'd have the unpleasant experience of being stuck in there for ages as Jenkins had closed his shop over the holidays. Now was the time to strike. He could never have a better opportunity for getting some kind of revenge.

Suddenly, he heard voices and the sound of feet walking down the alley by the hardware store. He drew back into a recess as a courting couple rounded the corner and he saw that it was Gwynfor and Mandy. Better and better, David thought grimly – the two of them might as well join the party. He noticed that they were not holding hands as they made their way over to the shed and Mandy tossed her head angrily as if they'd just had a disagreement. There was raucous laughter and knowing cries of 'Aye-aye!' as the door swung open and they joined the others. Gwynfor seemed to be in a temper and he slammed the door shut behind them. The impact caused the oil lamp to tremble alarmingly on the window sill and the metal bar fell into place with a clang.

"Look at what you've done now!" David heard Alex exclaim, "you've locked us in, you fool! Jenkins's shop is closed and we'll be stuck in here all night."

"Don't be such an old woman," Gwynfor replied. "Someone is bound to come along sooner or later."

"Cut us in on the next deal," Mandy said. "I've got some money to spend."

"There's no need to ask how you got it," Alex quipped.

"None of your cheek," Gwynfor said. "There's things little boys shouldn't know about. And you owe me ten fags, Alex, for doing you a favour."

"I've only got five left," Alex protested. "Anyway, she's left you now."

"It's a bit late for that smart talk, isn't it?" Gwynfor snapped and David could hear the annoyance in his voice. "It was you who spoilt things between Becky and me. Now give me those fags!"

"Why should I?" Alex asked insolently, looking round at his friends for support.

"I'll show you why!" Gwynfor exclaimed.

Despite Aeron's shouts of warning, the two of them wrestled in the middle of the floor, the oil lamp wobbled on the window sill and the next moment it crashed to the floor. Flames shot up into the air and the noise of argument was replaced by screams. At any moment now, the barrels of oil would be ignited and the whole place would go up with a mighty roar with them trapped inside. David stood there shocked, he had gained his revenge without lifting a finger and nobody could ever blame him.

The boys were desperately throwing their weight against the door but the iron bar held firm. David was about to turn and run for his life before the shed exploded when suddenly he saw Aeron's face between the metal bars of the window. Aeron's eyes looked pleadingly into his eyes. Cobwebs had settled on his hair like thorns and his face was haggard with fear.

David couldn't leave him there. He suddenly found himself running towards the shed and wrenching up the bar. The boys came tumbling out in terror followed by a tongue of flame and then they ran for their lives, all apart from Mandy, whose dress had caught on the nails in the wooden frame. She stood there screaming as her sleeve caught fire. David pulled up the lapels of his coat to protect himself from the intense heat and went in. He caught hold of Mandy and dragged her towards him with all his might. Her dress tore and the two of them fell out through the door. They got to their feet and started running but then the shed erupted, throwing them violently forward and everything went black.

Chapter 21

David didn't know where he was when he woke up. There were patterns of sunlight on a white wall and a hazy figure in uniform looked down at him from a distance. He was heavily drugged and felt himself drifting further and further away. It was his mother's voice which brought him hack to his surroundings but he didn't want to return to such a painful world. He tried to close his eyes to blot everything out.

"David darling, please don't leave us!" His mother's voice was shrill with anxiety.

David forced himself to open his eyes; he had to for her sake. He fixed his gaze on her and she caught hold of his hand, drawing him back into her world.

"Son, you're a hero." It was his father who now demanded his attention as he clasped his other hand.

How often had he longed to hear his father praise him but now he just wanted to be left alone.

"Since when have I been here?" he asked.

"You've been unconscious for more than a day, you and Mandy over there but it doesn't matter," his mother assured him. "The doctor says that you'll both make a complete recovery."

He turned his head painfully and saw Mandy smiling weakly at him.

"Thank you for saving my life," she mouthed, though no words came between her swollen lips.

"Your pals have been calling round often to ask if you're better," his father said, "and I know that they're waiting outside on the off chance that they may be able to have a word with you."

My pals, who are they? David asked himself.

"Isaac! David isn't strong enough to see them yet," his mother said firmly.

His father, however, had already gone to the door and the next moment Aeron, Alex and Stan trooped in.

"We've come to thank you for saving our lives, Dave," Aeron said. "If you hadn't come by when you did and heard us banging on the door, we'd all have gone up with the shed. You're the school hero and the headmaster will be holding a special assembly in your honour when you return to school."

"Hear, hear!" the other two chorused as they insisted on shaking hands with him, though he could barely grip the hands that were thrust into his.

"You could have been burnt alive when you went into that blazing shed to save Mandy," Stan said, "and because of your bravery Alex wants to say something to you, don't you, Alex?"

"Ah yes," Alex said reluctantly, as he received a sly kick on the ankle from Aeron. "School hasn't been the same without you and we want you, David, to join our gang when you come back."

David's father looked puzzled. "I always thought you were his mates," he said.

"No, what they mean, Isaac, is that they want David to join their bicycle gang," interrupted his mother. "You see, David, we've just bought a bike for you – instead of waiting for you to pass the Grade Four examination on the piano, as planned. It'll be there for you when you come home."

"So we'll be riding home together, Dave," Alex said. "But I tell you what, there's a new boy in our class called John Owen. He's from Casblaidd and I don't like the look of him."

"He thinks he knows it all and we'll have to take him down a peg or two," Stan agreed. "We'll get him on the way back from school."

"None of that nonsense, you two," Aeron said firmly. "Don't you dare forget that the last person you picked on proved to be the best friend we could have. Dave here risked his life to save us and I don't want to hear any more about hunting another man in the moon."

Alex and Stan looked away ashamedly while David gratefully touched Aeron's hand.

"You can visit me on my planet," David said kindly, "I shall keep a welcome for astronauts on the moon."

"That's enough for now, boys," the nurse said, as she saw the strained look on David's face. "Can't you see you're making him tired?"

"Sorry nurse!" they chorused.

As they were saying their goodbyes, someone rushed in past them.

"I want just one quick word with David," she said breathlessly. It was Becky, followed by Gwynfor.

"I knew you had it in you, David," she said. "You saved them all, including my Gwynfor," she added, giving David a resounding kiss on the cheek.

"Thank you for going back to save Mandy," Gwynfor said, "but what happened brought me to my senses and I now realise that Becky is the girl for me."

David looked over at the dejected Mandy who sighed and turned her back on them and he felt sorry for her.

David was pleased about being a hero like Jim Hawkins in *Treasure Island* but now he felt exhausted. Living up to his new image was hard work and he longed to be on his own.

"Thank you all for calling," he said, "but if you don't mind…"

"Of course not, my dear," his mother said, tidying his bedclothes. "You need your sleep and we'll call to see you tomorrow."

David was glad to see them go so that he could rest his head on the pillow and close his eyes. He said aloud the name of John Owen, the new boy in his class. He could help him so much.

He thought of those wonderful fish that he would be catching again in the Cae Helyg stream, the 'Head and Belly' fish and 'Bearded Jack', as they ventured out into the pools at evening. Then he dreamt of the fabulous shapes of trout beneath Cwmfferws bridge and the yellow frogs, which no longer seemed threatening. They now appeared lithe and sinuous, and he reached out a hand to touch them. All seemed bathed in moonlight as he fell asleep.

Also from Y Lolfa:

£4.95

DRAGONRISE
DAVID MORGAN WILLIAMS
dinas
An adventure
novel
for children

£5.95

£5.95

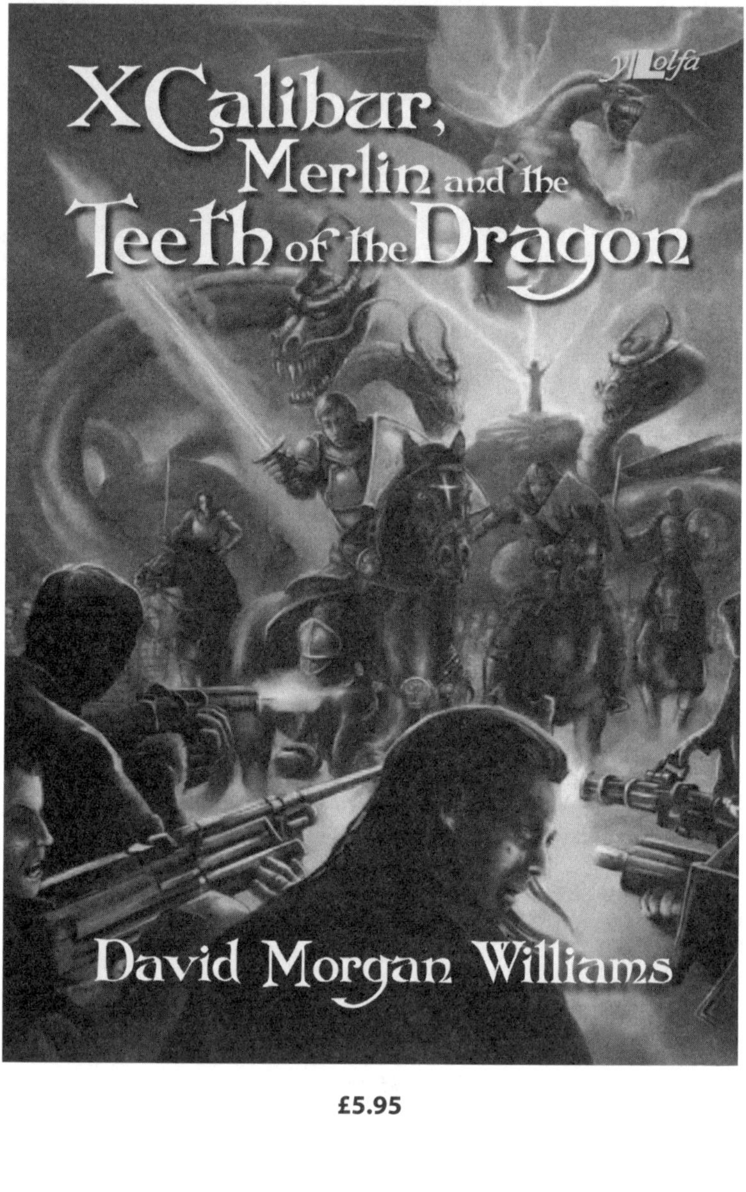
Y Lolfa
XCalibur,
Merlin and the
Teeth of the Dragon
David Morgan Williams

£5.95

TALYBONT CEREDIGION CYMRU SY24 5HE
e-mail ylolfa@ylolfa.com
website www.ylolfa.com
phone (01970) 832 304
fax 832 782